DEMONS AND DEVILS

Edited by
Stuart Young

Hersham Horror Books

Hersham Horror Books

HERSHAM HORROR BOOKS
Logo by Daniel S Boucher

Cover Design by Mark West 2013

Copyright 2013 © Hersham Horror Books

ISBN: 978-1492325758

All rights belong to the original artists, and writers for their contributed works.

All rights reserved. No part of this book may be reproduced, scanned or distributed in any form, including digital and electronic or mechanical, including photocopying, recording, or by any information storage and retrieval system, without the prior written consent of the Publisher, except for brief quotes for use in reviews.

This book is a work of fiction. Characters, names, places and incidents either are the product of the author's imagination or are used fictitiously, and any resemblance to any actual persons, living or dead, events, or locales is entirely coincidental.

Pentanth No. 4

First Edition.

First published in 2013.

Contents

Foreword
Stuart Young
5

The Abhorrent Man
Peter Mark May
7

Little Devils
Thana Niveau.
37

The Devil In The Details
John Llewellyn Probert
55

The Scryer
David Williamson
73

Guardian Devil
Stuart Young
107

Biographies & Story Notes
171

Hersham Horror Books

Also from
Hersham Horror Books:

Alt-Series

Alt-Dead

Alt-Zombie

PentAnth-Series

Fogbound From 5

Siblings

Anatomy of Death

Devilish Inspirations

Pentagrams. Black Mass. Sacrifices. Goat-headed demons. Chants to ancient evils. Just some of the things associated with black magic. And many of these images became popularised in the works of Dennis Wheatley.

He is best known for tales of black magic such as *To the Devil a Daughter*, but that is only the tip of his literary iceberg. Wheatley also wrote historical novels (*The Rising Storm*), thrillers (*The Sword of Fate*) and science fiction (*Star of Ill-Omen*). His Gregory Sallust series is rumoured to have been one of the inspirations for James Bond. In fact, the first appearance of the Duke de Richleau, Rex Van Ryn and Simon Aron was a non-supernatural thriller. It was only in the second book, *The Devil Rides Out*, that the Duke bothered to mention that he happened to be an expert on the occult. Wheatley himself learned of such arcane subjects through his acquaintance with Aleister Crowley aka The Great Beast. Wheatley denied ever actually studying the black arts with Crowley but he did own a copy of Crowley's *Magick in Theory and Practice* dedicated to Wheatley by the Great Beast himself. Crowley is rumoured to be the inspiration for Mocata, the villain in *The Devil Rides Out*.

Wheatley himself produced several essays on the occult as well as a non-fiction tome entitled *The Devil and all his Works* which, although not necessarily held in high esteem by "serious" students of the occult, is one of the main sources of research for Mike Mignola's *Hellboy*. And as editor of the *Dennis Wheatley Library of the Occult* series Wheatley reintroduced the reading public to authors such as Charles Williams, Lord Dunsany and William Hope Hodgson (a big influence on Wheatley's writing.)

So what approach have the authors in *Demons and Devilry* taken in tales of the occult as popularised by Wheatley? Peter Mark May's occult thriller has plenty of derring-do, exotic locations and historical detail among all the demonic goings on. Thana Niveau's tale of schoolchildren exploring a building site reveals dangers that aren't covered by Health and Safety. John Llewellyn Probert shows just what a depraved place Wales really is. David Williamson provides a blackly comic take on the pros and cons of the dark arts. And then there's my own effort which, in my totally unbiased opinion, should be lavished with the all the superlatives under the sun which I shall now proceed to do … Oh bugger, I've run out of room.

Stuart Young
2013

The Abhorrent Man

Peter Mark May

CARTHAGE: SPRING 146BC

Sandals and bare feet pounded along the sand and ash covered streets, on past burning buildings and fleeing women. Soot was flying through the air and blood lay on the ground in copious amounts, as the sacking of the great Phoenician city began.

On ran the two priests of Baal Hammon followed by their two spearman escort through the chaotic city, who were trying to flee the Roman slaughter. One held a cotton bundle in his arms, like it was a newborn infant.

Following at a distance were a century of legionaries, pushing and stabbing their way through the crowds of old men, women, children and animals.

"Run, you Macedonian dogs!" the Centurion goaded his men as they chased the priests through the back alleyways of Carthage.

One of the priests looked back over his shoulder: smoke and ruin dampening his eyes. Flames forty feet high circled and blazed from the burning temple of Aesculapius. He could not let himself think of the loss of his fellow priests or Carthaginians. They had a mission to fulfil, as the walls of the city fell around them.

On they ran and their pursuers followed deep into the small alleyways of the city, around a corner towards a small sacred temple.

A fellow priest was waiting outside, beckoning them in with all haste. Into the small domed temple they ran while the two guards turned to close the wooden doors against the invaders.

The priest at the door was helping the guards pull the doors too, when he was pieced through the gut by a Roman javelin. He fell to the pavement instantly killed by the precisely thrown weapon.

The Roman soldiers were nearly upon them, so one of the guards jumped out of the doorway to delay them. It gave his companion time to close and bar the temple doors behind him, as the Romans closed in for the kill.

The Carthaginian soldier's spear flew the short distance between them, felling the Optio running next to the Centurion. The shocked officer waved his men on, as he knelt to aid his dying comrade.

Two more Roman soldiers fell to the tenacious rearguard action of the Carthaginian guard and his short blade; before sheer weight of numbers overwhelmed him. When he finally finished his military career, lying dead on the temple doorstep, he had over twenty stab wounds about his body.

"Break down the door," the Centurion yelled, getting to his feet once more. Several Roman soldiers had gathered up a stone bench from a small garden at the left of the temple and were using it as a makeshift battering ram.

Demons & Devilry

The last of the Carthaginian spearmen watched as the doors of the temple bulged inwards with every charge from outside. He stood inside the outer corridor that ran round the length of the circular temple. He could do no more to secure the door, so ran halfway round the corridor's circumference to enter the inner sanctum of the temple.

This too was circular in shape and the ceiling domed, to prevent evil spirits from hiding in the corners. The last Carthaginian guard still alive in the city closed the decorative golden doors behind him, latching it shut. It would hold little protection from the Roman invaders, when they finally broke through the outer temple doors, but he would guard it with his last breath.

Meanwhile the priests had hurriedly opened a sacred casket which lay in front of a marble edged well, in the centre of the room. Out of the casket they took three rings of pure silver.

One priest hurried over to the last guard and thrust a ring into his palm. "Wear this, it will protect you."

The other learner priest of *Baal Hammon* undid the package of cotton, wrapped with salted rope, that he had carried through the city.

With an almighty crash the wooden doors splintered inwards from the onslaught of the Roman wielded stone bench. Led by their Centurion they poured into the round temple, splitting their numbers going left and right around the curved corridor.

Out of the cotton was unrolled a strange item. It was a blown glass bauble, large as a fist, which tapered down into a flat finished funnel. Only the round bauble like end was visible as it was wrapped in a protective leather sheath, with two copper bands clasping it in place.

The Abhorrent Man

"The Eye of Hannibal," whispered the guard in awe, but other events took precedence. The golden gate was kicked easily open and the Roman Legionaries poured into the round, domed temple.

The loyal Carthaginian guard felled one Roman with his spear, before sword thrusts to his upper thigh and right chest sent him falling to the marble floor, mortally wounded.

"Wait, you will doom us all!" cried the shorter priest, his arms wide in protest. The Centurion's blade detached his head from his neck in an instant.

The remaining priest raised the Eye in his right hand. The protective words had not been spoken and the Eye of Hannibal had not yet been purified.

All these thoughts were instantly ended, as a javelin thumped hard into his back, spearing him through his heart.

"Get the Eye," ordered the Centurion. This had been his special mission, entrusted to him by Scipio Aemilamus himself.

Two of the nearest Legionaries rushed forward to claim the sacred object, but the momentum of the javelin had pushed the priest half over the edge of the sacred well. As he died his hand lost grip of the Eye, which tumbled from his grasp into the waterless well below.

All the Roman soldiers had present held their breath as the Eye fell. Only a second of time passed and then came the breaking of glass at the bottom of the marble built well.

"Nooo!" cried the veteran Centurion in anguish. His dreams of promotion and an olive farm in Greece now vanished, like the Eye of Hannibal itself.

Suddenly the atmosphere in the inner temple

changed. The torches on the walls' flames turned from yellow to blue. The golden gates clanged shut and were held closed by some force that the Romans, both inside and in the corridor beyond, could not defy.

The Centurion, his Signifier and the other ten Legionaries raised their weapons, taking an involuntary step back from the well. Blood from the priest's corpse dripped from his elbow down into the black depths below.

The Carthaginian guard sat sprawled where he had fallen, his hands on his wounds. He had heard the rumours about the power of the Eye of Hannibal, but had not the faintest idea what was happening now.

A deep red glow was now rising from the well casting the entire temple in a blood coloured taint. The Centurion rushed to the temple gate to help try prise them open, but no soldier on either side could budge them.

The Centurion turned and fear filled his guts for the first time in his military career. Then everyone inside the temple stopped to listen.

It was distant at first and then grew louder; the unmistakable sound of galloping hooves. Louder and closer the echoing noise of the approaching horse grew, until it echoed around the temple wall with an almighty clamour.

Then, bursting forth from the well, leapt a large horse. The head, flanks, legs and tail of the horse were blood red and its saddle and bridle of reddish leather.

Sat upon this unholy steed was a soldier, his skin also red and his armour the colour of crimson. On his head rested a small golden crown. He carried no weapon, for he needed them not. His voice was the only weapon he required.

"Berith," whispered the wide-eyed wounded Carthaginian guard as he recognised the demon before him.

"Yes, I am Berith, Great Duke of Hell, released at last from Hannibal's binding entrapment."

The Roman soldiers were rooted to the spot, as the demon surveyed those in front of him.

"Yet I see in your weak minds that Hannibal is dead and my revenge is thus spoilt." The demon looked up upon the marble ceiling, its face set in thought.

"Such knowledge I gave you, Hannibal," the demon laughed. "What ruin lays upon your city now."

A spear flew from outside the gates at the demon. It entered the flank of his red horse, yet flew out the other side with no hint of damage. "Then I shall seek revenge on those whom have slain my worshippers."

The Romans both inside and outside the inner temple screamed in terror. The ones outside continued screaming as they ran for their lives, while those inside would never scream again.

Only the dying Carthaginian spearman held onto life long enough to witness it. Protected by the silver ring the priests had given him. He began to laugh as his eyes grew dark and Berith joined in with him.

It took until the sixth tortured captive priest to tell Scipio what he wanted to know. He and his subordinates, all wearing rings of silver, entered the temple of Baal Hammon.

Two guards quivered in fear at the golden gated entrance to the inner temple. A strange red glow dominated the round-domed inner sanctum, emanating from the lip of the well in the room's centre. Yet this did not take the air from Scipio Aemilamus's lungs, he who was Proconsular Imperirum and the great sacker of Carthage. There, standing in various positions around the temple, were twelve Roman Legionaries frozen in death, ordered by Scipio himself to capture the Eye of Hannibal.

Outside the temple the afternoon sun and the burning city made Carthage a scorching cauldron. Yet inside the temple of Baal Hammon Scipio stood gazing at the Centurion and his men who had all been turned to clear statues of purest ice.

Only the dead priests and a single city guard lay on the bloody floor unchanged by Berith's wrath, but all were dead. Scipio stared at the impossible sight, and then bid a hasty retreat from the temple.

"Slay every man; sell the woman and every child under the age of twelve into slavery," he ordered his generals.

Scipio got onto his horse and stared at the dome of the temple before him, still feeling cold inside even in this impossible heat.

"Raze the city until nothing larger than the size of a pebble remains. Except this temple, just bury that in sand so it becomes a tomb. And when that is done, salt the earth so nothing will ever grow here again."

Scipio's orders of total destruction and eradication of a culture were carried out to the letter and nothing grew or rose from the salt ploughed ruins.

*

The Abhorrent Man

GUILDFORD ENGLAND: SPRING 1924: THE SOCIETY FOR SUPERNATURAL RESEARCH'S HEADQUARTERS

"You quite sure you are up to this trip?" Inspector Morris asked his fellow Society Founder.

"It will be like a holiday I assure you my good man," replied Doctor Marsden from his wing-back leather chair, as they sat in the large estate's library.

"So who is this man that has invited you to his archaeological dig site then, may I ask?" Morris enquired breathing in the aroma of his brandy.

"A professor Louis Philippe. We met in France after the war and became firm friends. I wrote to him last year asking him to join our little society and he readily agreed," Dr Marsden explained taking a sip of his own brandy.

"I vaguely remember now. So how many other foreign members do we have now?" Inspector Morris asked with a sarcastic grin.

"Three as you well know, Benjamin. Louis; Franklin in Boston and Limesceau in Romania: it's a start." Marsden grinned back at his fellow Society founder.

"No race, no sex, no creed, no class, no religion or idolism shall interfere or gain any favour in the Society of Supernatural Research," said both men and then laughed.

This had been the founding promise of Morris and Marsden's Society. Your Society rank was the only thing that mattered in their eyes. The lowest and youngest man or woman born to the poorest family could outrank an Earl if his journey to the Inner Circle had progressed further.

Seven rings from the newest Initiate to the Inner Circle would determine your Society rank and nothing else. Their membership was growing every year; they now had thirty-two members on various circles of experience on the research of the occult and the evil things that lurk in the dark corners of the world. Which meant every year their files and investigations grew; all of them located at their headquarters in Guildford, Surrey at Dr Marsden's family home for seven generations. He, having no heirs, donated it to the Society.

"One day Benjamin, I envisage a whole worldwide network of Society members in every corner of the globe. Able to investigate the slightest supernatural and occult occurrence at the drop of a hat," Dr Marsden enthused, staring up at the ceiling, his thoughts in a higher plane.

"Are you sure you shouldn't be High Councillor and not I?" Inspector Morris asked, as Marsden always seemed to think on a more grandiose scale.

"No, my dear Morris, your command of men and organisational skills vastly outdo my own."

"So when do you leave?" Morris asked draining his glass: things would not be the same without Marsden around.

"In three days time - from Southampton to *Les Ports Puniques* in Tunisia - I cannot wait," beamed Doctor Stephen Marsden. He was looking forward to some sun, adventure on foreign soil and meeting his old acquaintance again.

*

The Abhorrent Man

LES PORTS PUNIQUES FRENCH PROTECTORATE OF TUNISIA 1924

Doctor Marsden knew had made a mistake with his attire as soon as he strode up on deck. The African sun beat down on Tunis and the passenger ship Marsden stood upon, in the overbearing heat. Apart from his hat his clothes were too dark, made of heavy materials, and his waistcoat was very much surplus to requirements.

It was too late to change now, his luggage was in the hands of the stewards and his cabin vacated.

"Best foot forward, Doctor," he muttered to himself walking slowly down the gangplank into a different world. The sights and exotic smells of Tunis, plus the chatter of French, Arabic and some English merged into one loud clamour.

Dr Marsden exhaled because of the dizzy heat, gripped his walking stick for dear life and moved off into the throng.

A small monkey ran over his brown polished shoes, which caused him to halt on the spot. He stared through the crowds of traditional robed Arabs and Berbers, sailors and French merchants; at a loss on what to do next.

Then out of the crowd a small man, in a linen jacket, fedora hat and cool looking cotton trousers, grasped his arms with delight.

"Stephen, *mon ami*." The man kissed each of the startled doctor's cheeks. "Welcome to French Tunisia."

"Louis," the English doctor finally recognised his old friend. "I'm so awfully glad to see you." Marsden was relieved now to find his old acquaintance who would know the lie-of-the-land.

"Let us find your luggage then we shall go to our hotel," Professor Philippe said leading his colleague to a steward on the docks. A young man in kneelength high brown boots, jodhpurs and only a white shirt, tagged along behind them, accompanied by two Arab gentlemen.

"Why are you dressed like that? Aren't you hot?" Louis asked, as Marsden handed over his ticket to the steward, as the two Arab men collected his luggage.

"Frankly I didn't know what to wear," Marsden explained. The nearest to the equator he had been before was Rome. Dr Marsden took out a handkerchief and mopped his brow and neck.

"You English, always dressed up for a dinner party." Louis smiled without any malice and behind him the young man laughed.

"Excuse my manners, this is Alex Lipton, a photographer from New York City." The two older men turned round and Lipton and Marsden shook hands.

"I found him wandering the Cisterns of Malga a few months ago quite penniless," Louis explained. "I needed a photographer so I took him under my wing. As you see, he has terrible dress sense also."

All three men laughed and they made their way through the crowds to a truck parked by some cargo pallets.

"Your carriage awaits." Louis Philippe beamed and lifted off his wide-brimmed hat.

Doctor Marsden stared at the dusty looking truck and exhaled, this indeed was going to be some adventure.

Lipton drove as Marsden and Philippe sat together on one large seat beside him.

The Abhorrent Man

"The perfect thing about investigating the ruins of Carthage is you do not have to trek miles into the desert to find it. It's on our hotel doorstep," Louis said to his old friend as they drove through the city.

They arrived at a place called Byrsa Hill, as their hotel was situated by the *Cathedrale St. Louis* and the museum of Carthage.

Their hotel Villa Didono was a pleasant enough place and Marsden was glad to get to his fan cooled room. A bed covered with what looked to Marsden like a huge net curtain dominated his room. He quickly flung off his jacket, his waistcoat and rolled up his sleeves. It was eleven in the morning now. He was to meet up with the Professor and young Lipton at twelve for a light lunch. Then on to visit the site Louis had been so excited about.

A knock at the door brought one of the Arab men from the port. His name was Abdul. He brought with him a cotton suit and a more suitable hat for the doctor.

"*Merci*," Marsden said to Abdul, who smiled and left the English doctor to change.

Marsden laid the suit and hat on a nearby table, heading for the balcony. The exotic sites of the outskirts of Tunis, built over the ruins of ancient Carthage, took his breath away. He stared long at the Cathedral; the roads and small white square houses, built up on each other like a child's set of blocks.

"Travel does broaden the mind." He smiled and breathed in a lungful of hot air.

His travels to Romania, France, Germany, Spain and Scandinavia were so different to this. Mainly because it wasn't raining or cold, but this was a whole different continent. He could feel the ages of history that lay buried in the sand and earth below him.

He could all but imagine the great Phoenician city sprawled out in front of him, built hundreds of years before the birth of Christ. Marsden stepped back into his room to wash and change his clothes, to match his changed mindset.

Marsden sat down in an ungainly fashion on the cushions before the low dining table. Next to him was Lipton and across the table were Philippe and Abdul. A vast array of exotic food was laid before them.

There were French bread baguettes, an oily soup called Charba, something called a *Brik a' l'oeuf,* salad and a mixture of lamb and *kefta* meat dishes. On the side were a sort of *ratatouille* with chickpeas and a bowl of dates, figs and peaches.

"When in Carthage," Marsden said staring at the food. He dove in, taking as many different dishes onto his plate as he could manage. He refused the wine and coffee offered and settled for a glass of water as he and his new acquaintances tucked into their lunches with their rights hands with gusto.

"So?" Marsden finally said. "Your telegram was rather cryptic, Louis. Why should your new excavation site interest me?"

"There is no need to be, how you English put it, coy," Louis replied. "You are among friends here, Stephen. Alex and Abdul would like to join me in your Society also."

"Well, you better begin then." Marsden was excited at the prospect of new and diverse Society members. He

The Abhorrent Man

and Morris's vision was of a vast network of three men Society teams in all the major cities around the world, made up of every race and walk of life.

"Before its fall Carthage had many huge temples to their gods," Louis began. "Yet what we have found is a very small fully preserved temple not far from here on some wasteland." Louis paused to pop a date into his mouth.

Lipton continued Louis's story as the professor digested his date. "On a Phoenician copper plate is a detailed map of the city of Carthage. It's held in the museum across the way. On that map is marked a small round building named only as the Well of Binding."

It was Lipton's turn to politely pause now by drinking his wine to allow the Professor to continue.

"Now in one hundred-forty BC an ex-Roman veteran of the Third Punic war, now a Quaster, described the fall of Carthage. He wrote of the search through the fallen city for the Eye of Hannibal, by Scipio's men." Louis picked up another date, knowing his good friend Doctor Marsden would ask the next and most important question.

"What was the Eye of Hannibal?"

"The Scrolls of Jerba say that Hannibal trapped a powerful Djinn inside, whom he used to see the future and would answer truthfully any question asked of him." All around the table grown men listened to Professor Phillipe like children at a story telling.

"That's how he defeated the Romans in battle after battle," Alex Lipton added.

"Though Hannibal could win great victories, the Eye could not tell him how to rule his people and who to trust," Abdul said, speaking for the first time.

"Genies in bottles, sounds all a trite Arabian Knights

to me; not to be rude." Doctor Marsden sat back a bit and looked at his fellow diners.

"As in all myths, some elements of fantasy and truth can be told together," Louis said with a friendly smile.

"Another legend tells that the Eye could not be used by any other man after Hannibal's death in one-hundred-eighty-three BC and it was kept by the priests of Baal, hidden somewhere deep in the city." Alex Lipton said, a frown forming on his young American forehead. "And what could be deeper than a well?"

"After the fall of Carthage the Eye of Hannibal is heard of no more throughout history." Professor Philippe sat back and ran his fingers through his hair.

"You say the temple you have found is round?" Marsden asked, trying to gain all the relevant facts.

"Like a dome, with an outer encircling corridor. We have excavated most of this and should find the entrance to the inner temple any day now," Philippe replied.

"A rounded dome fits with the binding of demons and devils, it gives no corners or shadows for the summoned spirit to hide in." Doctor Marsden explained, before taking a sip of water.

"Why a well, Doctor?" Lipton was eagerly consuming every word and fact that the two older learned men imparted.

"Could be symbolism. The well could signify the way out of the underworld," Marsden mused, chewing his bottom lip.

"Now," Louis clapped his hands together in delight, "I shall take you to the temple site."

"Excellent." Marsden smiled excitedly. This was what he had left England for; a different kind of

The Abhorrent Man

adventure, far removed from the damp ghostly sightings and Werewolf hunts in the Home Counties.

"We won't need the truck, it is but a five minute walk from 'ere," Louis explained to Marsden as the doctor started towards the vehicle.

"Thank the Lord for small mercies," he smiled back. A walk was better than sitting on that spring-less passenger seat again.

The four men from different countries set off down the hill a little ways, towards the excavation site.

Dr Marsden was glad of his borrowed suit and hat, walking next to Louis, his walking stick his only real English accessory. Professor Philippe led the way tying a neckerchief as he walked. Lipton, with his large camera around his neck followed and Abdul in his simple, but cool djellaba brought up the rear.

The site, next to some housing, wasn't the romantic image Marsden had envisaged on his sea voyage. It was boarded off by a high wooden fence and the earth looked like orange clay. He had expected deserts and oasis, with palm trees and pyramids, all he got was a large hole in the ground in the outskirts of Tunis.

The temple as they approached did look impressive though, in a simplistic way; surrounded by piles of grainy white sand.

"Looks like you had to move a lot of sand. Was it buried deep?" Marsden asked as they stopped at the lip of the excavation.

"It took many weeks, but that is not sand, it is salt," Abdul said from behind the doctor.

"Salt, really?" Marsden's mind was ticking over again.

"Yes, Doc. We had two feet of dirt, three feet of sand and then five feet of salt. I haven't seen anything like it apart from the lakes of Salt Lake City." Lipton said, raising his camera and taking aim at the temple below.

"Come, Stephen. Let us go in, eh?" Louis clapped his friend on the back gently.

Lipton led the way down an earth slope that zigzagged once. This was where the salt had been taken out of the dig by wheelbarrows.

Marsden had a similar feeling to when as a lad he first visited Stonehenge. That before him was a full-stop in the annals of history, something he could touch that was over two centuries old. What tales the very foundations of these places could tell, if they could only speak.

Half the temple side nearest the doors had been fully excavated, while the rest was being dug out by local Tunisian workers.

"Attention," one such man said to Marsden, rushing up to offer him a thick winter coat, in the eighty degree heat.

"*Non, merci.*" Dr Marsden fanned both out-turned palms at the man, who like a trinket seller in a bizarre was still trying to foist the coat into his hands.

"Stephen, put on the coat. You will need it, *mon ami*," Professor Philippe advised and Marsden turned to see him donning a similar coat. Lipton and Abdul had

The Abhorrent Man

also put on thick overcoats, and started to enter the dark, door-less entrance to the round temple.

Dr Marsden gave up and let the man put the coat on him and button it up. Marsden then thanked him in French before hurrying over to join Louis, who was lighting an oil lantern.

"I feel slightly overdressed for the occasion again," smiled the Englishman, with a twinkle in the wrinkled corner of his eye.

"Hot, eh?" Louis smiled back, handing Marsden the lantern. "You'll be glad of it in a moment. In you go."

"Why? Is it dirty in there?" Marsden asked as he passed into the dark threshold of the temple.

"Yes it is, but that is not the reason for the coats," Louis replied, entering the temple corridor behind him. "We go right."

The corridor was round and headed off left and right in both directions. From the sunlight coming from the entrance and his lantern Marsden could see the left way was still unexcavated five feet in.

Marsden headed right, following the back of Abdul coat with his lantern. To his surprise each step he made into the corridor the temple temperature seemed to drop ten degrees.

By the time they had made it round to where two Arab diggers were working on clearing the inner entrance to the temple Marsden could see his cold breath in front of his face.

"Why is it so cold Louis?" Marsden asked, shivering from the dramatic temperature loss.

"We are not sure," Professor Philippe tried to explain. "It could be the stones of the temple or the salt over it or if there is a well in the inner chamber. Or it could lead to an underground stream fed from the sea."

"It's a mystery ain't it, Doc?" Lipton stood huddled in the cramped corridor, next to Abdul and out of the workers way.

"We brought a thermometer down 'ere last week, it showed minus five degrees Celsius. It is as Lipton says, a mystery." Louis Philippe turned and frowned at his old friend.

"These men can only work twenty minute shifts before their fingers become too cold to work," Abdul said, pointing to the golden gates ahead.

The digging to open the gates into the inner temple had been proceeding slowly for over a week now. The gates opened inwards, so the workers had to dig under the gap at the bottom of the gates. A wall of salt blocked the entrance entirely. So the diggers had to clear a space into the salt drift, dig up and then clear, dig up, and then clear. The Professor did not want the ornate gates damaged or cut from their hinges, so the process was painfully slow.

"Attention," cried one of the diggers. As he plunged his spade up into the half cleared salt drift the whole pile suddenly shook and then collapsed. Luckily Abdul and the other digger pulled the man free from harm's way. After the dust clouds settled, everyone gasped. The drift had broken into pieces around their feet and now the gates were unblocked, leaving the inner temple visible for the first time in well over two centuries.

Lipton pulled a battery torch from his coat pocket and clicked it on as he approached the gates.

"What in sweet Jesus is going on?" he exclaimed as his torchlight picked up the impossible sight inside. The two diggers saw what was inside also. Yelling in panic they pushed passed Marsden and Philippe in their fearful escape from the temple.

Abdul was rooted to the spot in fear, as Philippe and Marsden approached the gates to see what the uproar was about.

"*Sacre Bleu!*" Professor Philippe exclaimed in nervous wonderment.

"It's impossible!" ejaculated Dr Marsden. Yet this was not the first impossible sight he had witnessed since forming the Society.

There in the torchlight, standing as they were two thousand years ago, were twelve ice figures of Roman soldiers. They were standing in various positions, heads turned towards a marble edged well in the very centre of the inner temple. All had expressions of terror etched for eternity on their open mouths and ice-cold lips.

Lipton's torch scanned around the temple from floor to ceiling. Three other figures lay in the room, not made from ice, but the mummified remains of corpses left in the positions they died. One was right on the edge of the well, one headless at the feet of a Roman and one slumped up against a wall like he had fallen asleep and never woken up.

"Photograph everything, Lipton. Quickly." Professor Philippe came at last to his senses. "We must document it all or no one will believe such a sight existed."

Lipton raised his camera, sending an eye-stinging flash shot across the temple and ice soldiers. Professor Philippe then opened up the latch of the golden gates and pushed them open with squeals of protest from the hinges.

Professor Louis Philippe, head of archaeology at *Universite de Marseilles*, was the first mortal to enter the inner temple, since before Christ was even born. He carefully walked around the ice legionaries, with Marsden and Lipton following after him. Abdul stood at the gates and looked in, but that was as far as he would allow himself to go.

Lipton moved across to photograph the slain Carthaginian spearman as Marsden headed for the well. Professor Philippe pulled a looking glass from his coat pocket and moved his lantern close to the bare arm of one of the ice Romans.

"*Merde*," he swore, because on the arms of the Roman solider were ice hairs and a long scar. Who in their right mind would sculpt in such detail? How had these figures not melted into water, having been buried in the sands of North Africa for two millennia?

Marsden knelt by the mummified corpse of the priest by the well, a Roman javelin protruded upward from his desiccated ribcage. The priest's skin had greyed and sunk in places, but was amazingly well preserved for being over two thousand years old. A small casket lay before the marble raised lip of the Well of Binding, inside lay several silver rings. Marsden picked one up to examine it.

A flash made everyone jump, but it was only Lipton taking pictures of the ice Legionaries up close.

"I fear, my friend Marsden, these were once living men." Louis claimed standing now next to the ice Centurion.

"No way, Professor. How can living breathing men be turned to crystal clear ice?" snorted Lipton as he moved around the temple.

"Are you a God-fearing man Mister Lipton?" Marsden asked, leaning over the well and dangling his lantern down to see if the bottom was visible.

The Abhorrent Man

"Yes sir, a Presbyterian born and raised," Lipton replied proudly.

"Then in the Bible is not Lot's wife turned into a pillar of salt?" Marsden stated. He frowned; he was sure he could see something glinting at the edge of his lantern's illumination further down the well.

"But-," Lipton began.

"Damn it," Marsden interrupted as the lantern slipped from his cold grip and fell, to smash with a flamed burst at the bottom of the well.

"Are you all right, old friend?" Louis asked, coming closer to the well, where Marsden lay next to the long dead priest.

"I thought I saw something down the well," he explained.

"Abdul, fetch some rope," Louis asked of the Tunisian man, who was glad to get out of the freezing temple for a few moments.

Professor Philippe knelt down beside his friend at the well's edge. The flames of the lantern below had died down now, but a reddish glow was emanating from the bottom of the well.

"What is that glow?" Professor Philippe asked his learned friend, his face now cast red by the crimson light that was creeping up out of the well.

"I fear we have woken something that no mortal man should ever witness," Dr Marsden stated.

"That's a horse!" Lipton exclaimed in shock as he heard the faint sounds of a galloping hooves. The unmistakeable equine noise grew louder in the round temple, echoing off the walls and the whole place was awash with red light.

"Quickly man, take this." Marsden grabbed another

silver ring from the casket and pushed it into the Frenchman's right palm.

He was about to reach for another ring for Lipton, when he and the Professor were thrown back from the edge of the well by some unseen force.

A shot of flame erupted from the well and as one, the two century old ice legionaries melted away into pools of water in an instant. Out from the well broke forth Berith the Great Duke of Hell, upon his red stallion. The horse stood over the well and the red skinned demon adjusted his golden crown.

Alex Lipton in fear, his brain working in automatic, raised his camera to take a picture of the red demon.

"You'll not entrap my soul again," Berith roared and pointed a black nailed finger at Lipton. Red fire engulfed the young American from head to toe, like his blood had turned into accelerant.

He felt only an instant of pain as the invading flames burnt his body down into ashes in an earthly second. He and his camera were gone from this world, snuffed out like they had never existed.

Both Professor Philippe and Dr Marsden looked down upon Lipton's untimely demise with dismay. Louis trembled with mortal fear, grasping the silver ring in his palm for all it was worth.

Dr Marsden saw it was his duty to end this: he after all had co-formed the Society to investigate these very occurrences of the supernatural and demonic.

Holding the silver ring in his right hand, he rose on shaking legs to confront the demon from hell.

"Demon, my actions may have awoken you once more; now I give thee licence to depart back to the Seven Hells, without rendering further harm to another living soul. Begone, I say, you are released from this prison and duly exorcised, Berith!"

Berith wailed aloud and all redness departed from the inner temple. Down back into the well the red stallion was being sucked by some unnatural gale, with the helpless demon upon its back.

Berith's last trick was to lunge from his saddle at Marsden. The shock of the attack caused him to drop the silver ring from his grasp and the demon gripped onto his left wrist like a vice.

Down, back into the well Berith was sucked and with him dragged in after him went Doctor Stephen Marsden. Louis flung himself at his friend, but missed grabbing his outstretched hand by half an inch. Both demon and Doctor disappeared down into the well.

Abdul had returned to see the last few seconds of what had transpired. He ran into the now silent and gloomy temple, with a length of rope over his shoulder. He helped the Professor to his feet as both exchanged scared and shocked glances.

"Where is Monsieur Lipton?" Abdul asked, his lantern rose high searching for the American photographer.

Silently the blanched faced Frenchman pointed to the pile of ash, on the temple floor.

"May Allah protect us?" Abdul muttered as he stared at the mound of ash, which when he had left had been a living breathing man.

"The well, Abdul. Quickly, tie the lantern to the end of the rope and lower it down. We must see what is down there."

Reluctantly, the Berber man did as he was asked and he and Philippe peeked over the side as he lowered the lantern down.

The lantern went down thirteen feet before it neared the bottom. There they could make out the crumpled figure of Dr Marsden.

"Quickly, get some strong men; we must go down to see if he is alive or dead." Louis shook the arms of the Arab urgently. Abdul left the temple again and managed to threaten and bribe four men into the temple. The day was waning now and dusk was falling quickly over the outskirt of the Tunis dig site.

In the end Louis had to go down the well on a rope, holding another line for the unmoving Marsden. The Tunisian diggers found the inner temple less frightening and cold now, but none were foolish enough to go down the well.

Finally, Louis reached his friend. Standing over him in the cramped conditions he reached down and felt at the Englishman's wrist for a pulse. Marsden was unconscious, but still alive.

"He has a pulse," Professor Louis Philippe cried with joy and began to tie the other rope around his friend. "Lift him up."

Abdul and the men above began to pull the brave Doctor up and out of the well.

Philippe explored the floor of the well as his friend was pulled up, above him. In the salt and sand, he found only a hand sized glass disk. Could this be all that remains of the legendary Eye of Hannibal?

He pocketed the glass and was intensely glad then to be pulled out of the god-forsaken place.

Abdul was standing over the laid out body of Marsden, as Professor Philippe was pulled from the well, by the four diggers. He gave each of them a silver ring

The Abhorrent Man

from the casket as both reward and protection.

"How is he?" Philippe asked, coming to crouch over his friend, to the left of Abdul.

"It is a miracle he has no broken bones or even alive at all," Abdul said, looking into the Frenchman's eyes.

"Let us hope he has not suffered any trauma to the head." Professor Philippe pursed his lips grimly.

Outside the sun set in the western deserts and night came to the French Protectorate of Tunisia.

In the inner temple, Marsden's eyelids flicked suddenly open and instead of his brown irises, they were as black and inky as the Abyss. Marsden sat up, his pale English skin now red as blood. Abdul and the Professor scrambled back away from the abhorrent man before them.

"Do not touch him, the rings will protect you!" Philippe screamed at the frightened diggers, who retreated around the other side of the well.

Marsden, possessed by the evil spirit of Berith, jumped to his feet and ran from the inner temple. Grabbing torches and lanterns Philippe, Abdul and the four diggers ran after him.

They found him outside the temple trying to escape. He stood at the slope of the dig site, but could go no further as the excavated salt blocked his escape. Salt was in the earth below, in large mounds around the site and scattered everywhere on the ground.

He did not notice Abdul creep up behind him, his demonic eyes staring up at the night sky, so close to freedom after so very long.

Abdul picked up a nearby spade and brought it crashing down on the back of the demonic Marsden's head. He fell to the ground in a heap, where Abdul bound him with salted rope and dragged him back into the temple.

*

GUILDFORD: EARLY SUMMER'S MORNING 1924
SOCIETY HQ (CELLARS)

Inspector Morris, Professor Philippe and Abdul stood outside the specially constructed cell in the cellars of the Society Headquarters. Morris flipped open his fob-watch and read the time, then checked it against the grandfather clock that stood next to the cell door.

"Five o'clock," he said and as he did the Grandfather clock began to chime five times.

The Professor also checked his watch and nodded at the Society's High Councillor.

Morris took a large iron key from his jacket pocket and put it into the lock of the thick oak door. The lock clicked as he turned the key and he pulled the heavy reinforced door open. It revealed a large brick walled cellar and in its centre was a cage measuring ten foot, by ten foot, by ten foot. The bars were made of hollow iron, plated with silver. Inside the hollowed out bars and sealed in was water from the Dead Sea, which had been blessed by the local bishop.

In this barred, iron, salt, silver and holy water cell lay Doctor Stephen Marsden on a single sheet-less cot.

"Stephen." Morris tapped on the bars and coughed loudly.

Marsden's brown eyes flicked open and he yawned, pushing out his arms in front of him.

"Is it morning already?" Marsden remarked as he sat

The Abhorrent Man

up on his cot bed and looked at his three visitors.

"Five o'clock old chap," Morris smiled back.

"Five o'clock eh? No chance of a lie-in then?" Marsden yawned again and stood up.

Professor Philippe moved forward and pushed a copy of the Holy Bible through the bars. Marsden walked over and grabbed it firmly with both hands. Professor Philippe nodded at Abdul, who came forward and unlocked the cell door with another iron key.

"How much time do I have today then?" Marsden asked, grabbing his clothes from a nearby chair and beginning to dress as his friends waited.

"Until at least half-past eight old friend. And we have much work to do today." Morris smiled and handed Marsden his shirt.

"Thank God for the long summer days and short nights." Marsden tried to smile as he pulled on his trousers. He was secretly dreading the winter and the cell where he would spend most of his time.

"Even rainy English summers?" Louis joked and patted his back.

"Every waking hour as a man, after being that abhorrent demon of a thing every night is precious my friends. So what is on the Society agenda for today?" Marsden asked, finally finishing getting dressed and grabbing his jacket off the back of the chair. Abdul led the way out of Marsden's nightly prison and the other gentlemen followed.

"A spot of early breakfast, then a little day trip, Stephen." Morris replied following Marsden out of the cellar.

"A daytrip eh. Anywhere nice?" Doctor Marsden asked, his interest piqued. "Brighton perhaps?"

"Werewolf sighting in Thames Ditton," Morris replied as the three men and the abhorrent man went upstairs, where Mrs Tingle was preparing a hearty breakfast.

The Abhorrent Man

Little Devils

Thana Niveau

"You're not supposed to go in there!"

The kids stopped at the torn chain link fence and Arabella shot her sister a scathing look. "You squeal, you little horror, and you'll be sorry."

Pippa drew back, aghast. Clearly she'd thought she could influence the older kids, though whatever delusion had made her think that, Arabella couldn't begin to guess.

They all stared at her, Freddie with his eyebrows raised comically, Scarlett with her arms crossed, looking bored. William slung his school blazer over his shoulder and crouched down to look Pippa in the eye.

"Look here, Pips," he said, using the nickname they all knew she despised, "there's six of us and only one of you. Do you really think we'd let you get away with telling tales on us?"

"Yeah," Rupert put in. He gestured theatrically towards the building site. "There's a lot of wet cement around here. A little girl like you could fall in so easily."

"Just like someone in a gangster picture," Freddie added, rubbing his hands together.

Arabella grinned smugly at the terror on her sister's face at that but Georgie looked worried.

"You oughtn't tease her so," she said with a frown. "She's only little."

But Pippa didn't seem to appreciate the older girl coming to her defence. She glared at them. "You lot are only twelve!" she blurted out with surprising boldness.

William gave her a tight smile, then took hold of her school tie and pulled her in close until they were nose to nose. "And if you want to live to be twelve yourself," he growled, "you'll shut your mouth and be grateful we let you tag along at all."

That got to her. Pippa's eyes filled with tears and her lower lip quivered. For one moment Arabella almost felt sorry for the little brat.

Scarlett heaved a dramatic sigh. "Such a bore. Now she'll start bawling."

"No she won't," said William, still smiling coldly at Pippa. "Will you, Pips?"

The six-year-old shook her head, blonde plaits swinging. She swallowed loudly and got control of herself, glancing fearfully up at her big sister as if seeking confirmation that William meant business.

Arabella merely gave her a withering look. "Honestly," she snorted, "you're such a baby." Then she turned on her heel and followed Freddie and Rupert through the opening in the fence.

Scarlett went next, after only a moment's hesitation. "The place is probably crawling with rats and spiders," she said with a shudder, pressing closer to Rupert.

The boys looked excited by the prospect but Arabella wished she hadn't said it. It was only likely to terrify Pippa more and if she ran off and told their parents where they'd been they'd all be for it. Then Pippa would really suffer. Oh, yes.

Georgie hung back, eyeing the fence uneasily. "I'm not sure this is such a good idea," she said. "Daddy says you can catch diseases from workmen."

Scarlett shrugged. "Please yourself." She looked only too happy for their little group to lose one of its female members.

"Aww, come on, Georgie," Freddie said. "We'll protect you." He snatched up a length of metal pipe from the ground and brandished it like a sword.

Georgie smiled but shook her head. "No, I think I'll leave you to it. I've got my riding lesson this afternoon anyway. See you."

Freddie tried one last time to persuade her but she clearly wasn't keen. Georgie waved goodbye as she turned and walked away down the street. Pippa watched her go, looking as though she regretted snapping at her. Now her only advocate was gone.

That'll teach you, Arabella thought.

William brought up the rear, grabbing Pippa by the wrist and hauling her through the gap. Arabella flushed a little at the thought of William taking her arm like that and then brushed the image aside, embarrassed. Once Pippa was inside the fence she ran to her sister and Arabella reluctantly allowed her to clutch her hand. Now that they were stuck with her they couldn't afford to let her run off.

The others had already disappeared into the half-finished building. It looked like the skeleton of a house, with sheets of torn milky plastic flapping against the sides like loose skin. A rude picture was spray-painted on one wall of a nearby Portakabin, along with a girl's name and a phone number. Underneath this were other scribbles and weird symbols. Possibly it was some language used by the gypsies who passed through the area in their battered caravans, only to be turfed out again.

They'd often seen scruffy kids from the comprehensive school playing on the site and once or twice they'd seen the police there. It was a place their parents and teachers had warned them to stay away from, a place nice people didn't go.

She heard a dramatic shriek followed by laughter as Scarlett no doubt clung to Rupert for protection from the creepy-crawlies inside. It had been Rupert's idea to go exploring and Arabella suspected that Scarlett had gone along merely so she could sneak off into a dark corner with him. As for herself, she'd gone because of William. Then bloody Pippa had tagged along and spoilt it all. It would serve her right if she stepped on a rusty nail.

Pippa's grip tightened on her hand as Arabella picked her way carefully across the rubbish-strewn site, following the laughing voices of her friends. There was the rattle and clank of empty beer bottles as the lads kicked them around and then laughter as one smashed against something. Arabella could imagine Pippa totting up the damage in her little head, like some horrid school monitor.

When they reached the house she made Pippa let go. Her own hand was clammy now and she wiped it on her pleated skirt as she frowned at her sister. The builders had left a mess behind. It looked like they'd had some kind of party. In addition to the beer bottles there was a scorched area on the floor where there had obviously been a fire.

"Ugh, squatters," Scarlett said, nudging the charred wood with the toe of one polished shoe.

"Looks like they had a barbecue," Rupert said. "Probably nicked a lamb from Harlow Farm and cooked it."

William peered closely at the remains of the fire. "A cow more like." He pulled out a long scorched bone and held it up for everyone to see. Strings of blackened meat still adhered to the bulbous joint.

Freddie turned to Pippa with a look of cruel glee. "Or maybe it's the bones of a little girl who wandered in here one night."

Pippa whimpered and clutched at her sister's skirt but Arabella kneed her away roughly. She fell to the floor with a cry and immediately scrambled to her feet. Her right hand was bloody, pierced by a shard of broken glass. She stared at the sight in horror and Arabella knew that once she got over the shock she'd start to cry.

"Look what you did," she snarled, digging in her blazer pocket for a tissue and thrusting it at her sister.

"I'm bleeding," Pippa whimpered.

"Oh, for God's sake!" Arabella wasn't gentle as she plucked the glass out of Pippa's palm and threw it to the floor. "Now tidy yourself up and don't start crying or we'll lock you in that filthy toilet outside."

Pippa's lip quivered as she mopped up the blood but she managed to hold in her babyish sobs. The others were getting just as tired of her drama.

"I'm going upstairs," Rupert said. Scarlett immediately trailed after him.

There was a dead rat on the landing. It was lying in a dark brown stain and its head had been crushed. Freddie peeled it up from the floor by its tail and dangled it in front of Scarlett, who shrieked and ran to hide behind Rupert. The three boys laughed and Arabella felt Pippa shrinking back lest Freddie throw the thing at her. But he dropped it with his own cry of disgust when he saw the little white maggots wriggling in its mangy fur. He smeared his hands up and down the wall, leaving behind a foul-smelling greenish smear.

"Revolting," Scarlett said with a shudder. She took Rupert's arm and hurried up the second flight of stairs.

Arabella eyed the rat warily as she edged past. Something about it was wrong. The maggots must have been burrowing underneath the rat's body and Freddie had dropped it so that the maggots were on top now. They writhed in the rat's flesh with renewed vigor and several of them, dislodged in the fall, were bending and twisting on the dusty floor like tiny worms, blindly searching for the putrefying feast they'd been evicted from.

"Come on," Pippa whispered, tugging at the sleeve of her blazer.

"All right, all right!"

They came to the top of the stairs and had a choice of directions. Someday there would be doors here. The hall would be carpeted and the walls painted. Someone would live here. She could scarcely imagine how it would look when it was finished. Right now it looked less like a future home than a project that had been abandoned and left to rot for years. But they'd seen builders on the site that morning on the way to school. She recalled thinking how easy it would be to fall from the top floor onto the unforgiving concrete foundation below. What would it look like? How would it sound?

When she became aware of the strange silence she looked up. Everyone was watching her.

"What? What are you staring at?"

Scarlett looked uneasy. She chewed her lip and glanced at Rupert before speaking. "What was that you said?"

Arabella blinked in confusion. "Huh? All I said was: What are you staring at?"

"No, no, before that."

Puzzled, she glanced down at Pippa. "Did I say something?"

The look on Pippa's face told her she had and that, whatever it was, it hadn't been nice.

"It sounded like Latin," said William. The other two boys confirmed this with a nod.

Arabella laughed. "I don't know any Latin," she said. "And I didn't say anything anyway. You lot are hearing things."

But Scarlett wasn't prepared to let it go. "Arabella, you absolutely said something. And it sounded evil."

Bewildered, she turned again to Pippa. Her little sister had inched away, her expression corroborating the claim that she had said something weird. It sent a chill through her spine.

"I may have muttered something about the rat but that's all. I certainly didn't say anything evil. In Latin or French or even English. Now can we please move on?"

The others eyed her warily for a few seconds before relaxing. One by one they turned away and headed off into the various rooms of the skeletal house. Pippa seemed torn between her sister and the others but after a moment's indecision she stuck with Arabella.

"I don't like this place," she confided in a whisper, her voice full of hope that Arabella felt the same. "It smells."

That was certainly something Arabella could agree

with. "Yeah, it does."

What were they doing here anyway? Of course the boys wanted to explore the building site; boys were like that. And girls didn't have to sit at home and play with dolls and bake pretend cakes; that's why they were there with them. But really – what was the point of exposing themselves to this filthy old place with its charred bones and dead rats? Just because their parents told them not to go there? What if it really was dangerous? The rebellion hardly seemed worth the risk. Maybe Georgie had had the right idea.

She was just opening her mouth to suggest that they'd seen enough and they could go now when she heard the sound. She frowned and listened. From somewhere down the hall came the low murmur of voices. It sounded as though they were chanting.

Pippa's hand was immediately around hers like a vise and Arabella gasped at the pain as her knuckles were crushed. "Oww!" She hissed at Pippa to let go.

"I really really don't like it here," Pippa whimpered. "I want to go home."

Pippa's fear gave Arabella courage and she made a face. "Don't be such a baby," she snapped. "It's only the others trying to scare you." She'd been on the verge of saying "us" but she didn't like the thought of being left out of whatever game her friends were playing.

"Come on, Pippa."

She dragged her little sister along the corridor and turned a corner. A thick plastic curtain hung down in an archway at the end, where a door would one day be. It was streaked with mud and Arabella gave a shudder as she wedged her hands into the split and pushed the plastic to either side.

The voices were louder and as she drew nearer she thought it sounded like Latin. She didn't know any herself but she'd heard it spoken at church and in films. It must be what the others had heard and thought was her.

This room was warmer than the others and she realised why at once. Something was burning. It wasn't entirely unpleasant and it made her think of Bonfire Night. In fact, the strange figure slumped smouldering in the centre of the room might be a small ragged Guy. It looked like a scarecrow that had fallen from its crossbeam. Its clothes had been stuffed with leaves and mulch, the charred remnants of which spilled out from the sleeves of its splayed arms. Wisps of smoke curled up from the scorched clothes like steam.

But November was a long way off and she couldn't imagine what other reason someone would have for burning a Guy. It certainly hadn't been any of her friends' doing; she'd have noticed one of them carrying something that size.

She lifted her head to call out to William and her voice froze in her throat when she saw what was on the walls. All around her were weird symbols, like the foreign writing she'd seen scribbled on the Portakabin outside. The dark red smears and splashes looked like the finger-painting of a mad child. Some of the symbols she recognised: they were the signs of the zodiac. She saw her own – Pisces – and felt a twinge of apprehension without knowing why.

Her symbol was surrounded by other crazy scrawls and a large picture dominated the far wall. It was sketched in black and the light from the fire made it gleam like metal. It looked like the figure of a person with a deer's head. Or maybe it was a goat. But it was all wrong. The thing had wings and Arabella couldn't tell if it was meant to be a man or a woman. It looked male but it also appeared to have breasts. One arm was up and one was down, with the first two fingers of each hand pressed together and extended as though pointing.

The voices were coming from the next room. Pippa hung back, staying close to the plastic curtain and shaking her head as she stared wide-eyed at the burnt effigy.

Arabella took a deep breath and moved further into the room, where she found the source of another smell. Scattered around the base of the painted goat-thing were the mutilated bodies of rats.

She covered her mouth to stifle her cry of horror. They were in piles. Dozens of them. It was only once she saw them that she heard the drone of flies buzzing lazily around the corpses and realised what had bothered her so much about the other rat on the stairs.

She didn't know how long it took for maggots to devour something like a rat but she remembered vividly when their pet rabbit Hoppy had died last winter. It was Arabella's week to feed him and she had forgotten three days in a row. She didn't want to be blamed so she didn't tell Pippa or her parents that she'd found him dead. She'd left him lying cold and stiff in his hutch outside for the rest of the week so her sister could find him. When it was Pippa's turn to feed him Arabella followed, her stomach fluttering with morbid anticipation. The sight was even worse than she'd imagined. So was Pippa's reaction. She looked like something possessed as she screamed and sobbed hysterically and finally fled into the house.

Arabella felt a strange mingling of guilt and excitement. Finding Hoppy dead had been a nasty shock for her but how much worse must it have been for Pippa? She crept up to the hutch and peered inside, curious to see what the passage of time had done to their dead pet. What she saw made her stomach clench. Hoppy's body looked like it was melting, collapsing in on itself. And just underneath the fur was the ripple of living things eating their way out. One pale eye stared at her with silent reproach and she backed away from the hutch, whispering apologies as tears shimmered in her eyes.

The rat on the stairs had looked just the same. But how could it have been lying there dead for days when there had been workers here only a few hours ago? Wouldn't they have seen it? Got rid of it? And how could a fire be smouldering up here when she and her friends were the only ones on the site? All at once she felt watched. They were not alone. Someone else was here.

She turned slowly towards Pippa but the little girl was crouched on the floor, hugging her knees to her chest, her eyes glued to the image of the goat-man.

From the other room the chanting rose in volume, a chorus that seemed to contain more than just the voices of her four friends. She didn't want to go in there. But, just as with Hoppy, she had to see. The urge was powerful and she felt as though invisible hands were gently urging her through the open doorway.

The room flickered with the orange light from the candles spread across the floor. The billowing plastic walls made it seem like the room was breathing.

William, Freddie, Rupert and Scarlett stood in a circle, their hands upraised, their faces blank. Their mouths moved but the voices were not those of children. On the floor at their feet, in a circle of candles, was the largest book Arabella had ever seen. Larger even than the antique dictionary her father kept on a stand in the library at home. Her eyes were drawn immediately to the open pages and she gasped at the sight. The pages were crawling with maggots, as though the book itself had once been alive. Around the squirming bodies were the scratches, loops and swirls of some strange writing. And as she looked, the text began to move too.

Like tiny snakes the black lines of unfamiliar letters coiled and slithered over the pages, forming pictures that then melted into other images. She saw the goat-man again, crackling flames, a knife, a screaming mouth.

In the corner of the room a mass of shadows swarmed. At first Arabella took it for a pile of blankets. Then she saw the pale slender arm lying alongside it and her mind began piecing the image together. It was a woman, naked and dead. Arabella didn't need to look closer to know that the shadows were a cloud of flies, that the woman's body was also home to the writhing, hungry worms.

But that wasn't all. The plastic gave a violent rattle in the wind and the flies buzzed angrily, rising to reveal other lumpen shapes scattered around the dead woman. Boots and hardhats swam into focus and Arabella felt a scream gathering at the back of her throat as she tried to understand what she was seeing, what must have happened here.

The builders were dead too, mutilated just like the rats. Strange writing adorned the plastic above them, smeared in what could only be their blood. In the afternoon half-light it looked like jam.

She wanted to run. She wanted to go home and forget they'd ever come here. Whoever – or whatever – had done this was still here. But her legs didn't seem to want to move. She felt dizzy and weak, like she was going to be sick. Gradually she became aware again of the chanting behind her and she turned to see that the others had joined hands.

Slowly her legs began to move, but instead of carrying her away they took her towards the others. The pages of the book shivered as she approached and she became aware of a strange humming sound in her ears. She felt her mouth moving along with the rhythm of the chanting and she realised that the humming was her own voice. She had joined in, speaking the alien words.

William and Freddie turned to her, their eyes like those of blind men, milky white and unseeing. They broke the circle and reached for her. Arabella moved towards William as if in a dream. She understood that she was wanted here, needed. There was something she was meant to do. Something important. She let them take her hands and guide her into the circle, closing it once more. She was part of the ritual now, for that was what it was – a ritual. Just like in church.

She was only vaguely aware of her fear. A wall of numbness separated it from her in her mind. If she could break through and touch it she would be terrified. She would scream. She'd be able to run away. But she was cut off from her emotions as effectively as from pain at the dentist's. It was there and she was aware of it; it just couldn't reach her.

From far in the back of her mind came an image of Pippa, cowering on the floor in the other room and staring at the painting of the goat-man. Arabella could see him moving, stepping down from the smeared plastic and onto the bloodstained floor. His hooves clacked on the floorboards as he approached the little girl.

Part of her wanted to call out to Pippa to run but her body was as numb as her fear. Untouchable. Unreachable. She stayed where she was, part of the circle, chanting the unfamiliar words that felt as natural to her as breathing.

The goat-man crossed the floor, his wings flexing, stirring the dust. Pippa gazed up at him, wide-eyed and curious. Why wasn't she afraid? Why didn't she run?

She could see everything as clearly as if she were right there. The goat-man leaned down to Pippa and reached out his hand. Pippa gazed at it wonderingly for a moment before getting to her feet. She held out the hand she had injured and Arabella could smell the blood pooling in her tiny palm. It was bleeding a lot for such a tiny injury. Pippa cupped both hands and raised them up to the goat-man. He lowered his head and dipped his snout into the blood and Arabella heard the slurps and snorts as he lapped up the offering greedily.

When he had drunk his fill he raised his head and a deep cold look passed between him and Pippa. Arabella's eyes began to tingle, as though the vision was damaging her sight, blinding her. The room grew hazy but they continued to murmur the strange words, clutching one another's damp hands in their little circle. Beneath them the pages of the book fluttered and the text writhed, forming images that melted into other images.

Arabella saw the goat-man turn slowly towards the room they were in. Fear leapt in her chest but she could do nothing about it. As he made his way towards them Pippa followed.

Now the creature stood behind them. Arabella could see him in the pages of the book as though in a mirror. He regarded each of them one by one, then closed his eyes and tilted his head back, listening to their voices. Suddenly Arabella knew they were speaking his name, calling him, giving him strength. She tried to close her mouth, tried to silence the many ugly syllables that defined him, but she was completely cut off from herself.

From behind her came a laugh and a glance at the book showed her Pippa, an expression of savage delight in her eyes. She put her bloodied hands up to her face and smeared them over her cheeks, her neck, her white shirt and striped school tie. She smiled. Then she pointed towards the circle, at William specifically. The goat-man nodded.

Arabella felt William's hand tighten on hers for a second. Then he was ripped from her grasp, torn from the circle as violently as if a bomb had gone off in his face. He didn't make a sound as his body struck the plastic, splitting it open. He fell silently, hitting the ground outside with a wet thud.

Pippa ran to the corner of the room to see, grinning madly at the sight that greeted her down below. Then she scampered back to the goat-man's side and this time Scarlett was her choice. Arabella sought refuge in the encroaching blindness as one by one her friends were snatched from the circle and sent flying to their deaths.

When only Arabella remained her voice grew silent at last. Pippa stood before her, her face a crimson mask.

"He needed blood," she said simply. "The blood of someone innocent." Her voice sounded like the rasp of an old woman.

Arabella tried to speak but now no sound would come out.

"She wasn't innocent," Pippa said, jerking her chin towards the dead woman in the corner. "She said she was but she lied. And they—" she indicated the builders "—interfered."

Arabella stared at the pile of bodies, the unsatisfactory sacrifice and the slaughtered workers. The ones who had simply got in the way. Had they interrupted the original ritual, perhaps tried to rescue the woman? Who had killed them?

A soft laugh came from the shadows. Arabella could just make out a figure there, clothed all in black, his gaunt face gleaming like bone. He moved away from the wall and Pippa went to him, smiling, and took his hand. Then she turned to Arabella and her expression grew cold and pitiless.

"Everyone wants power and knowledge," Pippa said, still speaking in that strange other voice, "and everyone assumes they deserve to have it." She glanced over at the dead woman. "Unworthy whore. Ah, but then you came. You and your little friends. But only one of you was worthy. We asked. She accepted."

Listening to Pippa speak about herself like this was terrifying, as though she'd gone mad. Somehow she knew it was the cowled figure speaking through her. The goat-man stood beside her, a towering figure of evil, a monster of the kind she'd used to tell Pippa about to scare her. But this was no made-up bogeyman; this was real.

It took all her strength but at last Arabella managed to move. She took a step towards Pippa. For a second the little girl gasped in surprise, but then she got control of herself again. Her eyes gleamed unpleasantly bright in her gore-streaked face.

"Not bad," she said. "You could have been useful to us. Stubborn. Strong. But this one is stronger. Stronger than any of you. Oh, how the seeds of bitterness and resentment grow. How they fester. They ripen into such poisonous fruit."

Arabella tried to move again but she was frozen to the spot. She could only stare in horror at her little sister — what used to be her little sister — and the hideous goat-man she had revived and nourished with her blood. He held out his arms and Pippa stepped into his embrace. She reached up to stroke the goat head, running her bloodied hand down its filthy muzzle as though it were a pet.

The wind lifted the plastic and the candles flickered. Pippa had vanished, along with the goat-man and the cowled figure. Arabella looked wildly around the room but she couldn't see her sister anywhere. Then something drew her eye down to the book on the floor. There was a new image crawling across the pages. Another goat-like creature stood pawing at something on the ground with its cloven hooves. A girl lay in a pool of blood, her body a mass of injuries. The goat-thing was eating her flesh. It lifted its head from the book, casting frightful shadows with its horns on the makeshift walls. Their tips were covered in blood.

"Pippa," Arabella whispered.

The goat-thing smiled as the candles guttered and went out.

Little Devils

The Devil In the Details

John Llewellyn Probert

There are many unforgiving things in this world.

The sea along the West Wales coast can be particularly harsh - brutal even, when the weather is bad and the waters have a mind to be unfriendly. Frothing waves the height of the oaks that pepper the fields further inland lash at unyielding rock, scooping away shale and tearing at the land, pulling a little of it away with every hammering of merciless salt water. It is a slow process, this erosion of the earth, but the sea does not mind - it has all eternity in which to complete its task.

Cloaked now in the darkness of midnight, only the stars and the full moon above are witness to the onslaught that is currently being wrought upon a sheer cliff of wet rock the colour of charcoal that rises for over a hundred feet above the crashing waves below. It is a clear night, and the noise the sea makes can only barely be heard by those within the house that is perched only a few hundred yards from the cliff's edge.

The house, three storeys and eighteen rooms of gothic splendour, used to be further inland, but the relentless work of the waves below has caused it to find itself just that little bit closer to the cliff's edge than when it was originally built nearly two hundred years ago. Now there is nothing beyond the west wing of the house but a few hundred yards of weatherbeaten emptiness where nothing but wild grass grows, and nothing but wild creatures venture.

Beyond that is the yawning emptiness of the night sky above, and the vast and insatiable appetite of the black sea below.

The unkempt state of the grounds does not concern the owner of the house. Nor, on this night, does it concern those he has invited to share it with him. For tonight is special. Those stars are in an alignment unseen for many years, that moon has achieved the exact and appropriate state of fullness, and is at just the right angle above the house in which a meeting is currently taking place. The storm clouds are yet to gather, but if all goes to plan they will come at the utterance of a single word, providing the appropriate preparations have been made, the correct incantations spoken with appropriate pronouncement and accentuation, the correct symbols inscribed upon the floors and walls in the correct mixture of animal's and children's blood.

And then of course there is the sacrifice.

Since the new owner moved in a year ago a number of alterations have been made to the house, the most obvious of which is the roof. The clustered columns, crumbling spires and tiles of the middle section have been removed and replaced by an altogether different structure. Apparently there was some discussion regarding these alterations in view of the building's listed status, but a generous cheque to the objecting parties concerned, and an accident befalling the member of the

Welsh Assembly who would not be bought off, has meant that now the main part of the building's roof consists of a dome of highly polished glass. It is multi-paned in an array of different colours and hues, all constructed according to diagrams in the ancient texts the current owner keeps concealed in his secret library. To the casual observer, of whom since the building has been renovated there have been a total of none who have lived to tell the tale, the dome might be explained away as an observatory, an architectural quirk, or a place of prayer.

It is this last that is closest to the truth.

If anyone were to venture close to the house during the hours of darkness (a most unwise thing to do, as I am sure you realise by now) that dome would usually be difficult to make out. It would simply appear as a humped silhouette against the backdrop of night, as if the house had grow a tumour or was trying to cast off a body foreign to its design and construction.

Tonight, however, there are lights burning within the dome, the flaming torches casting pools of orange light that reflect off the stained glass, painting this unholy rooftop chamber with an astounding panoply of flickering colours. Again, the positioning of the sconces has been as a result of precise and painstaking mathematical calculation. Nothing has been left to chance. The owner is all too aware that the slightest mistake could result in catastrophe. He has already lost two disciples through experimentation gone awry, and while their bodies reside in a private asylum near Swansea, he knows their minds will never be recovered as they have become the property of beings no sane man would ever be able to behold.

Tonight, however, he is confident that he will succeed. That with which he wishes to converse knows

The Devil In The Details

nothing of forgiveness, or mercy. Indeed it understands little of human affairs and has little interest in them, except when the opportunity arises to acquire souls. Then it becomes interested. It becomes very interested indeed.

A deal is shortly to be made, the repercussions of which will not be fully realised by those present until it is too late for any of them.

There are many unforgiving things in this world, but the things that exist outside of our normal perceptions are the most unforgiving of all.

Maxwell Chantry's eyes glittered in the light cast from the flaming torches. His face, obscured by a cowl of scarlet velvet that was featureless except for two eye holes, bore an expression of triumph none of the thirteen assembled in the sanctification chamber could see as he raised the ceremonial blade. His gaze drifted for a moment to the heavy iron rings set into each corner of the granite block before him. The naked girl lying on the stone was unrestrained, a requirement of the ritual, as was everything else that had been arranged for tonight, but Chantry still felt a pang of concern that the soporific mixture he had administered to her half an hour before might stop working. Then the worry was gone. If the drugs did wear off, he had also hypnotised the girl into such a state of submissive acquiescence that before she realised what was happening it would be all over. For her, anyway.

As the chanting of words unheard by mortal ears in centuries reached a climax, Chantry gripped the ivory hilt of the curved, cruel-looking blade. As he did so the intricately arranged emeralds and rubies that had been set into the bone of the handle amidst rituals of their own dug unforgivingly into the flesh of his palm. Chantry spread his arms wide, threw his head back, and uttered the final words of the ritual, his breath hot against the silk lining of his mask, before looking down once again at the girl.

Her eyes were closed but he knew they were blue behind those pale lids. Her tiny lips, pursed slightly in her relaxed state, bore not a hint of makeup, nor did the rest of her face. Her long, flame red hair spilled over and down the stone behind her head, the tresses resembling streaks of blood in the shadowy firelight.

And now it was time for the real blood to flow.

Chantry brought the blade down with the surety of a man for whom such an act was the culmination of years of planning. The blade pierced the girl's creamy skin on the right side of her belly, just under the midpoint of the border of her ribs. Chantry aimed the knife upwards so the polished steel pierced the girl's liver, the part of the body traditionally regarded by the ancient Greeks to be the seat of the darkest emotions.

They weren't entirely wrong, either, thought Chantry as he withdrew the blade and waited as a crimson flow began to flood from the wound. For a moment nothing else happened. Chantry was on the verge of closing his eyes and praying for aid to a different demon in the pantheon, despite the dangers, when, all at once, the girl's blood began to change. Before the awed expressions of those gathered in the room, the blood that has been spilled began to lift into the air. At the same time its state began to alter. No longer liquid, the blood was now changing to a rust-coloured smoke that rose above the

The Devil In The Details

body of the girl, hanging in the air just inches from Chantry's face. As it began to swirl and coalesce, the smoke began to take on a shape that filled Chantry with a mixture of gleeful anticipation and appalling dread.

The figure was cross-legged, the muscles in its limbs so well defined that the apparition might have been an anatomical specimen. Long claws extended from both fingers and toes, curling in a way that was even crueller than the blade Chantry still held. The face was still little more than a nebulous cloud, the rudiments of horns forming from the substance that was still spilling from the dying girl.

The dying girl whose eyes suddenly opened.

Who saw the thing floating above her.

Who took a deep, impossible breath and uttered a long, drawn out and even more impossible scream.

The work of years took just seconds to dispel. Even as the girl drew breath the apparition began to shimmer, to lose its form, the delicately charged particles that made it possible for the demon to appear in this dimension already repelling each other and returning to their normal state.

Chantry could feel his insides turning to water as everything he had been working for vanished before him in little more than a puff of smoke. He relaxed his grip on the knife and it fell to the altar with a clatter.

The girl, still bleeding but very much alive, reached for the blade and sat up. She took one last look at the form floating above her, even more monstrous now that it was becoming distorted as a result of the ritual's failure, before, with a howl of insane agony, she began to attack her own face. The honed blade swiftly reduced her beautiful features to a red raw mess, and by the time

Chantry had wrested the blade from her the girl was unrecognisable. Low moans bubbled from the bloody and ragged hole that was her mouth as Chantry pushed the blade in again, into her heart this time. He made sure she was dead before pulling the cowl from his head and taking several large gasps for air. The tears on his cheeks were not for the bloodied mess that lay before him, rather they were tears of rage and frustration at his failed experiment. He threw the knife to the floor before his horrified coven and made sure to regain his composure before he spoke.

"The stars will remain the same for some time yet," he said eventually. "We may still succeed."

"I need a virgin."

Dr Patrick Masters put down his scalpel, turned his attention away from the writhing figure on the makeshift wooden operating table, and regarded the man who had just barged into his private domain with an air of disdain.

"At a risk of stating the obvious," he replied as Chantry peered through the dim gloom of the subterranean chamber in which the surgeon was conducting some very private business, "Aren't you wasting your time looking for one in Swansea?"

Chantry coughed. The smell in the crumbling brick-lined room was as strong as the rudimentary gas lighting was weak. "How on earth can you see to actually do anything in here?" he said.

The mutilated thing on the table groaned. Masters picked up a relatively clean-looking gauze swab, poured something noxious and soporific onto it from a large bottle of ribbed brown glass, and held it over what was

The Devil In The Details

left of the subject's face for ten seconds.

"He won't be bothering us any more," said Masters once the convulsions had ceased. "But to answer your question, this particular case doesn't call for the most precise of techniques. In fact the individual who provided me with the necessary funds for this particular assignment stipulated that I should produce the desired modifications with as little finesse as possible. Before I finally did away with the fellow altogether, of course."

"Of course." Chantry held a silk handkerchief scented with Hugo Boss to his nose. He had suspected it might come in handy when he had discovered Masters' current whereabouts. "Now, could we possibly discuss some business in rather less salubrious surroundings?"

Masters peeled off his latex gloves, undid the cord on the stout red rubber apron that had protected his black waistcoat, and rolled down the sleeves of his tailored white shirt, fastening each cuff with a link in the shape of a tiny gold scalpel blade.

"Seeing as the business you wish to discuss is hardly likely to be in any way legal," he said, taking his suit jacket from a twisted iron hook in the wall just behind him, "I would have thought this an ideal place in which to consider any requests you might have that you feel I could cater for."

"True," said Chantry from behind his handkerchief. "But the smell."

"Ah, yes." Masters looked back at the body on the table. "The poor fellow claimed he didn't have the guts to have an affair with the wife of my client. Fortunately I was able to prove him wrong before he expired. Unfortunately he ended up making rather a mess of himself when confronted with the proof. Nevertheless, I have no intention of being seen in public with a possible employer, so I am afraid it's here or nowhere at all." He gave Chantry a mirthless grin. "So for both our sakes hurry up and tell me exactly what it is you actually want me to do."

"Exactly what I told you just now," Chantry replied, hoping the after shave would retain its potency for a few more minutes. "A virgin."

Masters rolled his eyes. "And if you're going to persist in inviting witty remarks that I really rather consider beneath me, I see no reason why we should continue this conversation."

The doctor made to push past but Chantry stopped him. "I need you to make one for me." He said.

Masters stopped, a gleam of interest in his eye. "Go on."

Chantry spread his hands. "What else is there to say? I have need of a virgin for a certain... ritual; and as you quite rightly surmised, I am not in a position to simply find one roaming the streets of a major city in South Wales. I do, however, have a willing volunteer who is familiar with what I require and is willing to take the risks the procedure entails for the quite fabulous rewards that may be hers. There's just one problem."

"I see." Masters rubbed his chin. "Well obviously I'd need to take a look at her, to determine whether or not reconstruction of the area was possible without major grafting of tissue from elsewhere..."

"But you can do it?" For the first time Chantry's voice held a tone of desperation that did not go unnoticed by the surgeon.

"I can do it," Masters replied. "But are you sure that's what you need?"

The Devil In The Details

"What do you mean?"

"Well," Masters narrowed his eyes. "Ritual. Virgin. And you have that house out in Pembrokeshire that you turned into some kind of observatory despite it being several hundred years old and having listed status. I can guess what you're up to, and I had always assumed that the virgin in these sorts of things was meant to be as much symbolic as anatomically correct. Do you really think that stitching a bit of epidermal tissue over a natural orifice that isn't really meant to have it there anyway is going to be acceptable to whatever no doubt dreadful thing you're intending to conjure up?"

Chantry shrugged. "I only have a little time in which to complete that which I wish to achieve," he said. "All I need is for you to do what I am asking. I'm happy to pay whatever fee you quote, and as a sign of good faith I'll arrange for a box of your favourite Monte Cristo cigars and two cases of Perrier-Jouet champagne to be delivered to your address tomorrow morning."

"I no longer smoke," said Masters with a self-satisfied grin, "but make it three cases and we have a deal."

The house of Maxwell Chantry, two days later.

The stars are still right, the moon is a little less full, but not to the extent that it should affect the proceedings.

The same room, the same time, the same ritual.

The girl on the altar is once again naked, is once again drugged. She is somewhat older than the previous victim and with the years of her greatest beauty behind her, she has agreed to participate in Chantry's ritual in the hope she might be able to recapture her lost youth. It is but one of many claims Chantry has made in order to convince her to submit, both to the ritual itself and the ministrations of Dr Masters' scalpel beforehand.

Chantry is wearing the same red silken cowl, is gripping the same, cruel, curved dagger.

He speaks the words of power once more. The words that should conjure the mighty demon he wishes to do his bidding.

The knife flashes down.

The blood begins to flow.

And flow.

Soon the chill granite is covered in it. The sacrifice moans softly as her pale body gives up the last of her life essence to the unyielding stone.

Maxwell Chantry takes a step back, raises his eyes heavenwards, and waits.

And waits.

"It didn't work."

Dr Patrick Masters switched off the blowtorch and lifted the eye guard.

"How did you get in?" he asked.

Chantry waved a rusty-looking key. "The owner of a disused slaughterhouse can be tracked down, you know, and paid off. Even on a Sunday."

Behind them, the middle-aged man hanging naked from the meathook begged for his life once more. Masters tore a piece of heavy silver packing tape from the roll he had used to bind the man's hands and feet and applied it to his victim's mouth.

"That should keep you quiet for the moment," he said. "Of course that's what you should have done in court, isn't it?" He looked at Chantry. "My employer would have got six years if it hadn't been for a very accommodating young lady who was able to provide him with an appropriate alibi. Or should I say, a very inappropriate one."

Dr Masters chuckled at what was obviously a private joke. He put the blowtorch down. "I'm guessing you have yet to find success with that ritual of yours?"

Chantry nodded. "Nothing appeared," he said. "Not even a sausage."

"Ah, now, if you want sausages," Masters pointed to his latest victim and then to a large metal box on the other side of the room. A conveyor belt led into one side and on the other was a receptacle obviously intended for whatever unfortunate creature the machine was capable of grinding to a pulp. "If you wait a little while I might be able to help you there." The victim in the corner began to wriggle more than ever. "Oh stop that," Masters gave him a prod with the soldering iron. "That was just a joke."

"In case I haven't made myself clear," Chantry said, looking distinctly uncomfortable in the presence of all this torture that wasn't sexy or intended for the conjuring up of higher powers. "Your surgery didn't work."

"Nonsense," said Masters, picking up a hideous-looking automated corkscrew device and switching on its motor. He allowed it a few experimental, and very noisy, spins, before turning it off again. "The surgery was as good as could be expected under the circumstances. I warned you it probably wasn't going to be sufficient. Which does make me wonder what on earth you're doing here."

"I have one night left," said Chantry. "Tonight."

Masters took a long, slim, rocket-shaped piece of

shining metal from the table. By adjusting a screw on the right hand side spikes emerged from it before the entire thing split in half and opened up like the jaws of a crocodile.

"And what do you suggest I do about that?" Masters asked, applying a little bit of oil to the ratcheting mechanism.

"I have another willing volunteer," said Chantry.

Masters raised an eyebrow. "Really?"

"Yes."

"REALLY?"

Chantry's shoulders slumped. "Not really, no. To be honest this time I really was wondering if you might be able to rustle one up for me, or you might perhaps know someone who could."

Masters would have rubbed his chin in thought but his hands were quite bloody and he didn't want to take his gloves off. Nevertheless he put on a very thoughtful expression before looking over at his victim again.

"I don't suppose you're a virgin, are you?" he said.

The gagged figure nodded as best it could for someone suspended in mid air.

"I'm sorry but I don't believe you." Masters turned to Chantry. "He couldn't lie in court but he's very happy to make up any old bollocks now that his old bollocks are in danger of coming into contact with some of my friends here."

"Can you help me?"

Patrick Masters held up the rocket-shaped device.

"I have a lot to get through this afternoon," he said. "In fact I am just about to see how far this can go up my friend's bottom over there. I'll try and see what I can do but I'm not going to promise anything."

The Devil In The Details

"Thank you." Chantry's display of gratitude was almost pathetic.

"Don't thank me," said Masters, applying a hefty quantity of lubrication to the shining silver. "Pay me. A lot. After all, you wouldn't want to find yourself on the other end of this, would you?"

Chantry left to the sounds of several different and equally unpleasant noises, the likes of which he hoped never to hear again.

The virgin was delivered early that evening, along with an invoice that, Chantry noted, included the time Masters had wasted talking when he could have been getting on with torturing his Sunday afternoon victim.

She was a pretty little thing, Chantry thought, as a delivery man who must have been eight feet tall carried her into the drawing room and laid her on a divan upholstered in ruby velvet. He signed the forms and gave the man a healthy tip for his trouble (and to try and give a spark of life to the man's cold dead eyes). Once the two of them were alone, Chantry turned his attention to his prize.

She was naked beneath the grey blanket she had been wrapped in. Her wrists and ankles had been bound with what looked like red ribbon. Her blonde hair had been styled in ringlets and fell to her shoulders. He had no idea what colour her eyes were, as they were closed.

All his attempts to wake her were unsuccessful.

Chantry checked her pulse. To his relief it was good and strong. A drug, then? Perhaps Masters had used something similar to Chantry's own recipe. He hoped so. The victim would have to be at least partly awake for the ritual to be a success. It occurred to Chantry that perhaps he should check to ensure his cargo was...intact, but he knew it was unnecessary. The order had been satisfied upon a gentleman's agreement, and Chantry could tell from the educated, creative and overly sadistic way in which Masters had tortured his victims that the doctor was most definitely a gentleman of the old school. He could trust him.

Couldn't he?

A little later that night, Chantry stood in his observatory, appropriately robed and garbed, his disciples gathered, the girl naked and prostrate on the altar before him. He held the jewel-encrusted knife in his right hand and, while no-one was looking, he crossed the fingers of his left. He figured he was allowed to be superstitious because, after all, he knew that such things existed.

Once again the moon shone through the multi-faceted glass dome, spattering the proceedings with spots of different coloured light. Once again Chantry brought the knife blade down, piercing the liver of the barely conscious young woman.

Blood began to flow.

Upwards.

Chantry held his breath as a figure began to form in the air above him. As her blood drained from her body, so the form hovering over her became more substantial. First came a skeleton of blood red bone, followed by the creation of muscles, tendons and blood vessels around it. Finally came skin, as red as the rest of the tissues.

No, not finally.

Finally came the red suit, the red shirt, and the red

The Devil In The Details

tie.

To Chantry, Satan also appeared to be a bit chubbier than he expected. And had rather less hair. Nevertheless he bowed his head, spread his arms wide in obeisance, and paid homage to the deity he had summoned.

"Master!"

The blood red man seemed unimpressed.

"Master," Chantry tried again. "We who are humbly gathered here greet you and await your bidding."

There was an awkward silence that lasted about a minute. Perhaps, thought Chantry, the devil's tongue was still being formed. Eventually, the figure spoke. With quite a strong Welsh accent.

"Oh you do, do you? And what do you expect in return?"

Chantry, his head still bowed, thought it best to be honest under the circumstances. "Power, oh Master. Power and the wicked delights of this world, and the next."

The figure sniffed. "Yes," it said. "That's what I thought you might want. Well I'm afraid you're going to end up disappointed."

Before he knew what he was doing, Chantry stopped averting his eyes and looked at what was speaking to him.

With a pang of horror, he realised he recognised him.

"You're not the devil!" he spluttered.

"Did I ever say I was?" came the reply.

"But you're...you're..."

"Say it," said the figure. "Say my name. The name you gave to those bully boys of yours so they could bump me off and you could do what you wanted to this place."

Now it was the figure's turn to spread his arms wide. "Say the name of Arfon Prys-Jones, the Welsh Assembly member you had killed to further your own meagre ambition."

For the moment Chantry's tongue seemed to have failed him, and so he remained silent while the figure continued.

"You really should research those whom you intend to do away with, Chantry," said the satanic incarnation of Arfon Prys-Jones. "We black magicians aren't such an insular lot. A few discreet enquiries would have revealed that having someone like me killed is the very worst thing you could do. I do not forgive, Chantry - ever. When my wife decided to find solace in the arms of another man after my death I arranged for Dr Masters to teach him a lesson. In fact I believe you were witness to some of it. Even that nasty business with the blowtorch and that witness you paid to lie in court about what happened to me wasn't a good enough hint that I was after you."

"But...the ritual," Chantry spluttered, looking around him. "All my work. It wasn't designed to...bring you back."

Arfon Prys-Jones, black magician, late of the Welsh Assembly, recently endowed of a much greater power than could be bestowed by regional government, smiled very unpleasantly.

"Three women," he began. "Three women sacrificed during the cycle of the full moon on the grounds which I myself had intended to acquire for the purpose of praising His Most Mighty Unholiness. It didn't matter if they were virgins. All that did matter was that the last would be bound in the treated tendons of one who had killed for me."

The Devil In The Details

Chantry gulped. "You mean...?"

Prys-Jones' grin grew even broader. "I am afraid Dr Patrick Masters will never get to drink all that champagne you sent him," he said. "But if I were you, I wouldn't be worrying about that. In fact in a little while, you won't be worrying about anything at all."

Behind Maxwell Chantry, there was a shuffling noise as his ex-disciples began to close in on him.

"I'm glad to see they know which side their bread is buttered," said the more powerful of the two black magicians in the room. "I'm sure by the time they've finished with you I'll need to have this room redecorated. But then you always did have terrible taste, didn't you Maxwell?"

Chantry fell to his knees.

"Forgive me," he begged, as disciples that had become monsters used fingers that had become talons to tear at his flesh.

"I'm afraid I can't do that," came the tired reply. "There are many unforgiving things in this world, Maxwell. Unfortunately for you I happen to be one of them."

The Scryer

David Williamson

"Mr. Kelly? Mr. Daniel Kelly?"

The visitor was a short, weasel of a man in his mid to late sixties with a Bobby Charlton style comb-over the like of which Dan hadn't seen in many a year and a small, neat black moustache. He carried a battered leather briefcase in his left hand and proffered a laminated business card with his right.

Dan gave the card a cursory look, but sensed that this unwelcome caller was either from the council about the rent arrears or from the social services regarding his latest incapacity benefit claim.

Either way, the creep wasn't getting into his flat … not unless he had a warrant!

"Well…*are* you Mr. Kelly, or not?" asked the stranger, a somewhat peeved tone in his voice.

Dan held the door ajar just wide enough to speak through the gap.

"Who wants to know?"

The visitor thrust the card forward, so that it was directly in front of Dan's eyes.

"My name is Mitchell Pink. I'm from Plunkett, Pink and Wareham, probate solicitors – "

The Scryer

At the mention of the word 'solicitor', Dan slammed the door of his council flat in the face of the man and set the dead lock.

Almost immediately, the letterbox flap opened.

"I'm here as the bearer of possibly very good news, Mr. Kelly! I'm not after money. Rather the complete opposite, in fact!"

The shabby flat door remained closed for all of ten seconds, before its occupant opened it wide and ushered Mitchell Pink into the hallway.

"Okay, you've piqued my interest. What's this "very good news" you were talking about?"

Pink glanced around the tatty hallway, noticing the large pile of unopened final demands stacked on a side table, the peeling wallpaper, and the row of battered shoes carelessly lined up along the skirting. The place smelt of un-emptied garbage, grease and a general airless mustiness. The solicitor tucked his briefcase firmly beneath his arm.

"Is there somewhere…er….more comfortable we could speak?" he asked.

Dan smiled tightly and shook his head in disbelief.

"Nowhere you would think of as "comfortable", but the front room has seating, if that's what you mean?"

"That would be admirable, Mr. Kelly…please, lead the way…?"

Dan picked up the assorted scattered detritus littering the settee and dumped it over the back, out of sight.

"Take a pew." He couldn't help but smile as Pink's nose visibly wrinkled before he settled himself, uncomfortably, at one end of the settee, placed the briefcase across his lap and undid the clip holding it shut.

"Please…take a seat yourself, Mr. Kelly? This could

take some time…"

Dan Kelly sighed aloud, shook his head and sat in the armchair beside his unbidden visitor.

"So….what's this all about, Mr…….?"

"Pink…..Mitchell Pink."

"Okay, Mr. Mitchell Pink…I'm all ears…?"

The little solicitor cleared his throat, removed a buff coloured folder from his battered case, took out the wad of papers contained within, placed a pair of wire rimmed glasses on his prominent nose, and began.

"Right, Mr. Kelly….just a few formalities. Firstly, can you please tell me your date and place of birth?"

"Why? What's this all about?"

Pink shook his head and part of his careful combover fell across his brow making him resemble a balding Hitler look-a-like. Dan almost laughed out loud as the solicitor carefully eased his hair back into place.

"Please, Mr. Kelly. I assure you that if you are the *right* Mr. Daniel Kelly, this meeting will benefit you greatly. I need to confirm that I have the correct person….?"

Dan frowned.

"Okay, okay. I was born on the 31st of January 1969 in Isleworth, London."

The solicitor looked at his notes, nodded and gave the briefest of smiles.

"And your parent's names, please?"

"Thomas Arthur and Mary Janet…Kelly, naturally. Both now pushing up the daisies, alas."

Pink smiled tightly once more and scribbled something on the paper before him.

"And just to confirm; do you have any siblings…brothers or sisters? Any other relatives?"

The Scryer

Dan shook his head.

"Nope. I'm an only child and both my parents were only children as well. Not big breeders in our family! "

The solicitor nodded, removed his glasses and folded his hands across the papers on his lap, smiling excitedly.

"Well, Mr. Kelly…I am pleased to say that it would seem that I have traced the right man!"

Dan frowned and then shrugged.

"Oh goody-good. So now what? Have I won the lotto or has someone donated their kidneys to me?" he asked, sarcastically.

Pink smiled broadly.

"In a manner of speaking, *yes*, you have won the lotto, though you will have to sort out the kidney donation for yourself, I'm afraid." He chuckled dryly.

Dan raised an eyebrow and studied the little man seated opposite him.

"This is your lucky day, Mr. Kelly. A *very* lucky day, indeed!"

Kelly sat forward on his chair and nodded encouragingly.

"Right; I have to tell you that a distant relation of your's, your *only* relation so far as we can detect, died some months ago and has left a property as well as a not insubstantial amount of money."

Dan was now *very* interested in what his visitor had to say, and nodded enthusiastically for the man to continue.

The solicitor consulted his notes and then added.

"The property, I have not seen it myself I might add, is in Essex. And you, as the only surviving member of the family, are in the fortunate position to have inherited everything."

Dan looked in a state of shock. His eyes had grown wide and his mouth trembled slightly as the news began to sink in. Finally, he found his voice.

"*Essex*? I've never been north of the Thames in my life! *Essex*?" he repeated, still unable to fully comprehend the information he had just been given.

"I understand that it's quite a substantial property," continued the solicitor, as he looked around the grungy, cluttered lounge of the flat. "Certainly, it's rather larger than your …er….current accommodation."

As Dan Kelly sat there, shaking his head in disbelief, the front door to the flat opened and then slammed shut and two raised female voices could be heard arguing in the hallway.

"Don't speak to me like that, you rude little cow! I'm your bleedin' mother, not one of your scummy mates!"

"My mates ain't scummy…*you're* the scummy one!"

The two women were still bickering as they burst into the living room, and both stopped mid-sentence as they notice the diminutive figure of Mitchell Pink seated uncomfortably on the settee.

"Who the bleedin' hell is this? Not another bailiff…I *told* you not to let anyone in!" screeched the older of the women.

Pink and Dan got to their feet at the same time, Dan clearly attempting to silence his wife with a telling glare.

"It's nothing like that, Irene. This is Mr. Pink. He's brought us some unbelievably good news….."

The solicitor smiled thinly and held out a dainty hand.

"Pleased to meet you…erm….?"

"Sorry, Mr. Pink. This is Irene, my wife and this is our daughter, Kelly."

Pink looked a little baffled.

"Yeah, that's right, mister. Kelly Kelly – how bleedin' stupid is that, eh?" explained the girl, shaking her head furiously and glaring from mother to father as if they were the most stupid people on the planet.

Pink looked both dumfounded and a little embarrassed, and decided to gather up his paperwork, which he replaced inside his tatty briefcase, latching the lid shut once more.

"Well then, Mr. Kelly. I'll leave you to relate the good news to your family, and I'll be in touch within the next few days with all the details regarding the property etc."

"Property? *What* property?" demanded Irene, as Pink edged his way between the two women and out into the hall, only pausing to hand Dan one of his business cards before opening the front door.

"I'll be in touch shortly. Mr. Kelly…Ladies…" And with that, he was gone.

Dan closed the door and leant against it, not knowing whether to faint, scream or laugh hysterically.

The suspicious faces of the two women in his life brought him back to earth with a thud.

"Daniel Kelly…what the bleedin' hell have you been up to? And what was that weird looking bloke on about?"

A little over a week later, Dan, Irene, Kelly and Mitchell Pink were being driven in a hired car to a relatively remote area of Essex close to the border with Suffolk.

The driver, with some difficulty, located the property now owned by Dan and his family and pulled up outside a set of large, cast iron gates with sturdy looking brick pillars supporting their weight. Each pillar had a strange, gremlin-like character upon it and a paint-flaking sign attached to one of the gates announced that they had arrived at The Old Manor House.

"This seems to be the place," said Pink, with more than a touch of awe in his voice.

"Bloody hell!" replied Kelly.

Dan let out a long whistle as his wife merely sat there in dumbstruck silence.

The driver hopped out and opened the double gates wide, before easing his car through and proceeding along the overgrown gravel drive towards the Old Manor House.

Even Kelly remained silent as they travelled for some 500 yards before being greeted with the sight of a very large, timber framed building which clearly dated back to Tudor times, possibly even older.

The driver swept around the circular driveway and pulled up beside a set of great oaken doors, obviously the main entrance to the property.

He jumped out of the car and ran around to open the passenger doors.

Slowly, the occupants clambered out of the car and stood in silence, simply looking up at the huge old building in complete disbelief.

Finally, Kelly Kelly broke the silence.

"Yuk! What's that horrible *smell*?" she asked, and everyone sniffed the air and turned to look at the girl.

"I think you'll find that's the smell of the countryside, Miss Kelly?" suggested the solicitor, managing to maintain a straight face as he spoke.

"Pwoar! It's *disgusting!*"

Mitchell Pink shook his head in disbelief and then fished in his briefcase for the keys to the building, selecting the largest of the bunch, before stepping forward and unlocking the huge double front doors.

As they entered the building they were greeted by the smell of an old house which had clearly not been aired for quite some time. A similar smell to the Kelly's old flat, thought the solicitor. They should feel well at home here!

The wide hallway was panelled in finely detailed oak, the floor paved in its original heavy stone. Overhead, the ceiling was formed from beautifully ornate and detailed plasterwork, which seemed to be in amazingly good condition considering its age. Candle sconces, now converted to electricity, lined the panelling every few yards, and Pink flicked a light switch near the door turning them on to give a weak, pale yellow glow to the hall.

Ahead of them stood a huge wooden staircase, with thick handrails and bulbous, heavily carved balusters sweeping up to the floors above. The hallway itself extended for some sixty feet or so and the finely carved doors set into the panelling clearly led off to a selection of living areas.

The hall alone was probably twice the size of their entire flat back in south London.

Dan was completely stunned by the place.

"And...all this is *ours*?" he asked, incredulously.

The solicitor smiled. "Yes, Mr. Kelly. I can assure you that there has been no mistake. The whole house is yours – lock, stock and barrel – to do with what you will."

Dan let out a low whistle.

"Blimey! But how much does it cost to run a house like this? And all the grounds out there to look after, too…?"

Mitchell Pink rummaged in his battered old briefcase once more and produced an envelope which he handed to Dan.

"That is the full details of your inheritance, Mr. Kelly. I think once you've studied the figures, you'll be more than happy to realise that you can live here in comfort…providing that you do so using a certain amount of prudence?"

"Prudence?" asked Kelly. "Who the hell is she?"

The solicitor smiled patiently.

"I mean, so long as you don't blow the lot on race horses, fast motor cars, helicopters and other such frivolous items, you will have enough to live very well in this wonderful old house for the rest of your days."

"Oh!" she replied, simply.

The house came fully furnished and most of the antique furniture was worth a small fortune in its own right, so the only items they needed to allow them to move straight in were some more up to date appliances for the kitchen and a few other mod cons. Irene, perhaps understandably, insisted on all new bedding throughout.

"We don't know who this relation of your's was, what he died of or even where he died. I ain't taking a chance on catching something!" Which was probably fair enough, all things considered.

Kelly demanded the biggest flat screen television

they could find, but other than that, and the occasional moan about missing her mates back on the estate – oh, and the regular debate on whether all that fresh, country air was actually good for you or not – she seemed reasonably satisfied. At least, as satisfied as any seventeen year old would ever be.

Dan's distant relation, evidently some cousin several times removed by the name of Quentin Kelly, had employed a woman from the nearest village, which was some three miles distant, as a housekeeper, and she was soon re-employed to 'do' for the new residents.

Despite Dan's careful questioning regarding his late departed relative, the old woman had very little to say about him, other than the fact that he kept himself to himself, was a very quiet sort of gentleman and always paid her wages on time. He had few friends that she was aware of, although as she only worked until mid afternoon, she had no idea what went on when she wasn't there.

Their new life settled into a routine, and oddly, even though their previous existence had been a constant battle of trying to make ends meet with the odd bit of wheeling and dealing, never quite knowing where the next penny was coming from, Dan found himself getting bored.

Now that he could do anything he wanted to and had the money to enable him not to have to worry about bills, he soon discovered, somewhat ironically, that he didn't really know *what* to do with himself.

He had explored the majority of the house since they'd moved in some six weeks ago, but decided on a whim that he would have a poke around in the vast cellars which spread the full length and width of the manor house.

The housekeeper had told him that the Old Manor House had been built on the site of a much older, medieval building dating back to the 14th century and he considered it well worth a poke around to see what was down there.

Oddly, there was no lighting in the huge cellar. So, after a brief investigation with a small torch, he rigged up a series of portable lights so as to better see what secrets, if any, the place held.

For such a cavernous cellar, it seemed strangely empty. There were a few old tea chests scattered around near the bottom of the stairs, various bits of broken old furniture, a few suitcases mainly packed with mouldering ancient clothes, but very little else of any real interest.

The ceiling was of vaulted stone supported by thick stone pillars and there were several arched storage niches throughout, mostly empty. But at the far end, covered with a ragged, moth-eaten old blanket, he discovered a small, worked-leather trunk with a large ornate lock on its front.

Dan tried to lift the trunk, but it was heavier than it looked, so he dragged it the length of the cellar, back towards the lights and set about trying to open the thing. It was locked, obviously. Nothing interesting could possibly be that simple to open, now could it?

Then he remembered the bunch of keys which Pink had given him and headed back upstairs to fetch them.

No luck at all; none of the keys on the bunch looked even remotely as though they would fit the lock on the trunk.

Plan B was called for, and although the leather trunk

The Scryer

was clearly several hundred years old and no doubt worth a small fortune, needs must, so he took a heavy screwdriver to the brass lock and jemmied the thing open. It took a considerable effort, and Dan mused that they certainly knew how to make things that would last way back then.

Oddly, although the trunk was heavy, there was very little inside it. There were a couple of musty old leather bound books, one of which was wrapped in some sort of oilskin, a pair of what appeared to be silver candle sticks, some kind of weird hat, and lastly, buried beneath a mouldering cloth right at the bottom, a piece of badly tarnished metal with an ornate stand which would enable the thing to be stood upright.

There were also a handful of old coins, the like of which he had never seen before, but only made of silver or similar. So, no hidden treasure, bars of gold or diamond necklaces then?

He unwrapped the book which had been protected by the oilskin and idly flipped through the pages, which were not made of paper but rather some kind of skin. Vellum, no doubt.

The pages were covered in a spider-like scrawl and there were strange diagrams painstakingly drawn in the margins. The writing was completely unintelligible, at least as far as he was concerned. It was neither English nor any other language he had ever seen, not that he was any kind of expert of course, but he had seen some of the old Tudor age books in the library upstairs, and this scribble wasn't remotely like any of those.

He re-wrapped the book and shoved it his back pocket, when the light caught the piece of metal with the ornate stand and he spotted for the first time that it too had been etched with symbols and writing like those in the book, and he picked it up to study it more closely.

It was far heavier than it looked and he almost dropped the thing until he grasped it with both hands.

It was badly tarnished, but by adjusting the angle and the lighting, he could definitely make out the scratched symbols and strange writing. He decided that it might be worth cleaning up and, as he had nothing better to do, he hefted the thing against his chest, kicked the lid of the chest closed with his foot and headed upstairs.

"What the hell is *that* thing?" asked Irene, her face resembling someone who'd been sucking on a particularly sour lemon.

Dan placed the last wad of Brasso back into its tin and looked at the result of his two hours of labour. The whatever-it-was was now gleaming brightly and he could pick out far more detail on its carefully etched surface.

The stand was even more ornate looking now that he had cleaned it up, and he noticed that it had been moulded with the faces of goblins or demons. Whatever they were, they looked positively *evil*, but he found them completely fascinating and studied them for quite some time.

"I asked you what the hell *that* thing is? I'm not sure I even want it in my house!" repeated his wife.

Dan noticed his reflection in the now highly polished surface of the metal and realised for the first time that it was obviously an ancient mirror.

He had to force himself to look away as it seemed to be drawing him in somehow.

Dan turned to his wife.

The Scryer

"*Your* house? Since when did you have a rich relation who died and left *you* a mansion?" he asked, bitterly, staring her straight in the eyes.

Irene was not a woman who was easily flustered, but the odd look in his eyes unsettled her and rather than confront him further, she turned on her heal and stormed out of the kitchen.

Dan smiled to himself and returned to look at his find from the cellar.

Yes, it was definitely a mirror. A very fine mirror at that. It made him look…what? Different in some way? He appeared …what was the word? More handsome? No...not that. Dignified perhaps? Hmm, possibly? Knowing…yes, he looked more knowledgeable somehow. A man who knew what he wanted from life and how to go about getting it.

He *really* liked this mirror.

He was still seated at the kitchen table which was covered in newspaper and scraps of wadding when Kelly came home after visiting her old friends from the estate.

"What's that bit of old crap? You been out car booting again?" she asked, sniggering at her own wit.

Dan turned suddenly and stared at his daughter, a dark look in his eyes which shut her up immediately.

"You would be the one to know about crap, young lady. You have no idea of the finer things in life…just like your mother!" And with that, he snatched up his mirror and left the room, heading upstairs leaving his daughter lost for a retort for once.

Dinner that night was a very quiet affair, with Irene and Kelly casting one another questioning looks as Dan sat at the head of the large oak dining table, looking for all the world like a medieval lord waiting to be served by his wenches.

He didn't say a word throughout the meal, other than to ask why they were living in such a grand old house, yet still eating rubbish like pizza and chips.

"You always *liked* pizza and chips before we moved here and you started getting all high and mighty!" retorted his wife.

But he merely raised his hand to silence her and said, "That was when we didn't have the money for the finer things in life and didn't know any better. Things must change now that we're here…and change for the better."

The two women looked at one another and said nothing.

Shortly afterwards, the dreams started.

Night after night, Dan would dream the strangest things, with always a bearded man wearing a high ruff collar who had the most piercing eyes at the forefront.

He could hear chanting in the background in some unintelligible language, words that Dan could not even begin to imagine the meaning of. And the dreams always took place in the vast cellar beneath the house which was poorly lit by thick, fat candles which gave off a pungent odour.

For some reason, Dan felt a connection with the man in his dreams, almost as though he knew him somehow, as if there were some kind of a bond between them, a bond which extended through time and space.

In fact, the dreams/nightmares, call them what you

will, were so vivid that Irene had insisted that he move into one of the spare rooms so that she could get a night's sleep without him moaning and thrashing about in their bed.

He had agreed, rather too quickly, she thought and he now had the mirror in pride of place on his bedside cabinet and seemed more than happy not to be sharing the matrimonial bed with her.

Three days later, Mitchell Pink arrived out of the blue along with his partners Alistair Plunkett and Gordon Wareham.

"Hello, Mrs. Kelly," said Pink, cheerily as though they were old friends. "We were in the vicinity and decided to pop in and see how things are going with your new life? How are you settling in, my dear lady?"

If Irene Kelly thought that it was at all odd that these three men just happened to be "in the vicinity" she said nothing as she ushered them into the drawing room and called for the housekeeper to organise some tea and whatever else was going for her unexpected guests.

"Well," she began by way of a reply "It's certainly different from our old place, that's for sure! Not sure that Dan is enjoying it that much. He seems a bit …er….tense these days?"

Mr. Plunkett spoke for the other two.

""Tense." In what way is your husband "tense", Mrs. Kelly?" he asked.

Irene looked at the three solicitors perched on the edge of a large sofa and decided that they looked more like three old fashioned undertakers than men of the law, and she repressed an almost overwhelming urge to laugh out loud.

"I don't know how to describe it, really? He was fine until he started rummaging about down in the cellar. He's been a bit odd ever since then."

She couldn't help but notice the look which passed between the men, which although fleeting, worried her for some inexplicable reason.

Wareham was the next to speak.

"Would it be possible to speak with your husband, Mrs. Kelly…if it's not at all inconvenient, of course?" and the solicitors sat there, all three with identical expressions on their faces, with only Mitchell Pink carefully fussing with a wayward lock of his comb-over.

Just at that moment, there was a light knock on the door and the housekeeper wheeled in a trolley with the tea things. The woman smiled and nodded at the three men, almost as though she had met them before, but there was no acknowledgement from any of the solicitors.

After tea, Irene went and found her husband who was, as was often the case these days, to be found in his room staring blankly into the mirror beside his bed.

"Pink is here with his two mates. They want to speak to you…don't ask me what about. They give me the creeps!"

Dan snapped out of his reverie immediately.

"Tell them I'll be right down." he replied, dismissively and she left the room without another word.

"Ah, Daniel!" said Pink as Dan entered the room. "Allow me to introduce you to my partners in crime; This is Alistair Plunkett and my other colleague, Gordon Wareham. Gentlemen, *this* is Mr. Daniel Kelly."

A smile sprang to the lips of both men, and they thrust out their hands in greeting. They looked very pleased to make Dan's acquaintance, almost as though they were in the presence of royalty or the very least, a celebrity of some sort.

"Well then gentlemen, to what do I owe this honour? You lot, out here in the middle of nowhere? What can I do for you?"

It was Plunkett who spoke, clearly the senior partner of the three solicitors.

"A-hem...Well, it's not what you can do for us, Mr. Kelly...it's really more a question of what we can do for you."

Dan smiled warmly. "I would say that you gentlemen have done *more* than enough for me, already. Just look at this place for a start...I'd have still been living in that filthy hovel on a dreadful housing estate if it wasn't for you!"

Plunkett waved his hand dismissively and continued.

"Ah, but that was our duty...to find the last surviving heir to Quentin's estate. The very last of the bloodline, so to speak."

Their host looked puzzled. "Am I missing something here? I really can't imagine what more you could possibly do for me."

Mitchell Pink spoke now.

"Your wife tells us that you have been investigating in the cellar. Might I ask whether you've found anything of interest down there? It's a very old house, as you know...there must have been something worth discovering...?"

Dan could detect a faint nervousness between the men, an uneasiness in their manner which led him to believe that there was far more going on than he was able to grasp.

"Well, aside from several heaps of cra...rubbish and a load of broken furniture, there was this old trunk...?"

The look which darted between the three older men was too obvious to hide and Dan quickly took the opportunity to cut to the chase.

"So...what exactly, interests you gents in my cellar? Is it the book...or the mirror?"

Plunkett, who had risen to his feet, sat down heavily, and taking a clean white handkerchief from his jacket pocket, dabbed nervously at his brow.

Gordon Wareham spoke for the first time.

"It would seem that you have seen through our little deception, Mr. Kelly. We have, as they used to say, been undone!"

"Wait here, please...I have something to show you all."

Five minutes later Dan had the mirror and the book placed on the coffee table in front of his guests, and they sat staring at them in undisguised admiration...and more than that perhaps. There was an aura of fear mixed with anticipation hanging in the room and an almost fanatical gleam in the three men's eyes, particularly as they studied the metal mirror.

"Is *this* what you've come here to see?" asked Dan, simply.

The visitors nodded dumbly, barely able to tear their eyes away from the mirror, just as Dan himself had found it so difficult to do.

"Mr. Kelly...there are certain details that I feel we have omitted in our dealing with you. Important details which I should enlighten you with...and more so, now that you have discovered the Scrying glass."

"The *whating* glass?"

The Scryer

"This is no mere mirror. Please, let me start from the beginning and all will make sense, I hope."

Dan settled himself down into a chair opposite his guests.

"Please...tell all" he said.

"Have you ever heard of Doctor John Dee, by any chance?"

Dan shook his head.

"Well, he was a famous, perhaps infamous, gentleman way back in the reign of Queen Elizabeth 1st. He was, at sometime, her personal tutor in astrology as well as other arts. But, there was a darker side to the man. It was said that he was involved in necromancy, alchemy and 'other' black arts, the full extent of which we will probably never know."

Wareham paused to take a sip of his cold tea, before continuing.

"Doctor Dee, though clearly a very forward thinking and highly intelligent man – way ahead of his time – alas, had one flaw in his character. Although he was deeply involved in occult matters, he was unable to ... er, shall we say 'communicate' with the other side. For this, he needed an expert in that field. A Scryer as they were known. And the best of those Scryers was a man named Edward or Ned Kelley...."

A frown passed across Dan's face.

"Yes, Mr. Kelly...Edward Kelley is your direct ancestor. We haven't tried to work out exactly how many 'greats' are involved, but please take it from me, that you are indeed his descendant. His only *surviving* descendant, I might add."

The younger man looked nonplussed. Although he had never heard of this man Edward Kelley, he somehow thought deep in the back of his mind that he *knew* the man?

"What did he look like...this ancestor of mine?" he asked.

"Ah, that's easy" replied Mitchell Pink, smiling and delving into his ever present briefcase. "Here is a drawing of him from the time." And he handed the likeness to Dan.

Dan took the drawing and knew before he even set eyes on it that this was the man in his dreams.

Although he was half expecting to recognise the face, the reality shot through him like an electric charge and he found himself shaking, a cold sweat erupting across his brow.

The three solicitors were studying his face intently as he looked at the old drawing of Edward Kelley. Mitchell Pink smiled tightly and said, "You've seen this man before somewhere, I gather....?"

Dan closed his eyes, and nodded, handing the illustration back to Pink.

The older men looked at one another, satisfaction clearly evident in their expressions as the waited for Dan to reply.

"Mr. Kelly.......?" pressed Wareham.

Dan rubbed his face with both hands as though trying to wake himself.

"Yes...I've seen him before. In my dreams. He's been appearing every night in my dreams..."

"He's made a connection!" whispered Plunkett, triumphantly, to the others.

Their host suddenly opened his eyes and studied the older men, noticing their look of success and undisguised excitement.

The Scryer

"Connection? What do you mean I've made a connection?" he asked.

The solicitors were staring at Dan and smiling insanely.

"I mean," replied Plunkett "that you have made a connection with your ancestor...Edward Kelley. Edward Kelley, the original owner of the Scrying glass you discovered in the cellar. *This* Scrying glass." he added, reverentially touching the metal mirror placed on the table before them.

Dan shook his head.

"What the hell are you talking about? The man's been dead for what....four hundred years or so? How can I have made a "connection" with a dead man?"

"Four hundred and fifteen years, to be precise" interrupted Mitchell Pink, continuing "Ned Kelley was a very mysterious character, Daniel. It was said that he could, amongst other talents, turn base metals into gold. Indeed, it was this ability which ultimately led to his downfall, as he was imprisoned by Rudolf II of Bomehia who refused to release Ned until he had supplied the king with enough gold!"

"But what does all that have to do with him appearing in my dreams, for God's sake?"

"I'm coming to that, Daniel," continued Pink.

"As has already been mentioned, Kelley was involved in 'other' practices...especially when he worked with Dee. Necromancy was a very great interest of those men. The practice of communicating with the dead for purposes of foretelling future events, and discovering hidden knowledge....witchcraft as it was often called by the uneducated."

Dan let out a low whistle.

"So old Ned was a witch then?"

Pink smiled tightly.

"You *could* say that, I suppose? But he was also so much more than that; so much more than the typical depiction of witches in popular mythology. While others were healing the sick with their remedies and casting petty curses on those they disliked, Kelley was doing great works! And undoubtedly, via his Scrying glass, he is trying to contact you…his last remaining relative. As…erm…as we hoped would be the case, before we managed to track you down…."

Dan's eyes narrowed and he fixed Mitchell Pink with a piercing stare.

"So you *knew* all this stuff even before you met me?" he asked, incredulously.

The three solicitors looked sheepishly at one another, and nodded in unison.

"I'm afraid we did…yes." responded Pink. "The man you inherited this property from, Quentin Kelly, knew the whole story, but unlike you, he simply didn't have the 'gift'. Although we tried for many years to make contact with Edward Kelley, it never happened. Oh, we've tried many other so-called mediums, naturally, but we realised that it had to be a descendant …a direct descendant of Kelley himself. Fortunately, not only are you the last of the line, but you also possess 'the gift'!"

Dan's eyes narrowed again, but there was a certain look of dawning knowledge in his face now.

"I thought you told me that you'd never so much as seen this house before the day you brought me here?" he said to Pink, who had the decency to flush a deep red, before shrugging his shoulders.

"I'm sorry, Daniel. It seemed a harmless enough ruse

The Scryer

at the time..."

Dan pursed his lips and considered his position briefly.

"So, what are *you* lot after? Gold, I guess? You want me to contact old Ned to discover his secrets, then?"

"*No!*" shouted Pink "There is so much *more* to be discovered than just gold, Daniel! Ned Kelley had 'other gifts' which concern us more. Certain connections of his own...links to a much higher power, worth more than all the gold in the world to us and... other people!"

Dan was quick to spot the reference.

"Which *other* people?" he demanded.

Pink realised that he had said too much and looked nervously between the other two men. They were both glaring at him angrily, but the damage had already been done.

"If you expect my assistance, gentlemen, and you obviously *need* it, I want to know everything...and I mean, *everything!*"

Plunkett shrugged, resignedly, and said "Well, Mitchell...you had better finish what you've started?"

Pink nervously patted at his comb-over before speaking.

He cleared his throat and continued.

"We...that is the three of us, are part of a group. There are nine others within the group...your great uncle was the tenth before his demise. The group is made up of a variety of powerful men; businessmen, politicians, a police commissioner, a bishop...twelve in all. You, would naturally become the thirteenth member or our...er...coven, and would also, obviously, be the most important member, as you are the one with the 'gift'."

Pink paused to let Dan digest the information, before

continuing.

"We are all convinced that, with your assistance of course, we can communicate with Edward Kelley and hopefully learn all that he is willing to share with us…or rather, share with you? Knowledge that has been lost in time…things that will help to make our group become the most powerful men on the planet! You included."

The dream that night was the most vivid to date.

Dan was a bystander down in the cellar of the house which was lit by guttering torches fixed to the stone walls. There were a group of men each dressed in black robes, their hoods raised so that he could not see their faces. They were gathered in a circle surrounding a man seated at what looked like a stone altar with tall, black candles placed at either end.

The seated man was Edward Kelley, and he was staring intently at his Scrying glass, his brow etched with concentration, his dark eyes focused upon something which Dan couldn't see from where he was 'standing', beside one of the thick pillars which supported the vaulted stone ceiling.

Then, the circle of hooded men began chanting in a tongue which Dan could not understand. They appeared to be saying the same phrase over, and over , a phrase which started in low voices and which grew in volume until the whole cellar reverberated with the ancient words and Dan had to cover his ears to block out the cacophony.

"Nigrum Dominus, nos precor ostende te! Nigrum Dominus, nos precor ostende te! **"Nigrum Dominus, nos precor ostende te!"**

Suddenly, in his dream state, Dan found himself

The Scryer

standing directly behind his ancestor, Edward Kelley, looking into the Scrying mirror, seeing what *he* could see.

The surface of the mirror was cloudy looking, but the cloudiness slowly cleared and a face appeared on it's surface. A man's face.

Dan almost screamed aloud as he recognised the image in the Scrying mirror.

It was *his* face!

The strangest thing, if things could get any stranger, was the fact that his image in the mirror showed him asleep and in his own bed. His face was contorted and twitching, his eyes beneath his eyelids were rolling from side to side, proving that he was in a very deep sleep.

Then he realised with horror, that Edward Kelley had now turned to face him from his seated position at the altar. Indeed, *everyone* present in the cellar was now staring at him silently. The faceless, hooded 'congregation' had now stopped their chanting, but Dan found the total silence far scarier than the alien sounding words.

"Ah...he *sees* us!" said Kelley, triumphantly, rising slowly from his seat.

"We have made the *connection!*"

The screams had woken both Irene and her daughter, and they stood trembling and clutching one another on the threshold of Dan's bedroom, staring as he thrashed wildly about his bed.

Suddenly, he sat bolt upright, sweat dripping down his terrified face, his hair matted and damp, the duvet wrapped about his body holding him in an anaconda-like grip. He sat there, trembling and gasping for air like a semi-drowned man, his eyes staring, his lips twitching.

"What the hell is going on here, Dan?" asked Irene, nervously. "What's happening to you? You've never had so much as a bad dream in all the years I've known you, until we moved into this place!"

Dan shook his head, sweat flying from his hair and splattering his daughter's face, who wiped it off without thinking, too scared to speak or complain in her usual manner.

Her father's chin suddenly dropped to his chest and it appeared as though he had passed out, when he suddenly took a deep breath, releasing it slowly before speaking for the first time.

"I...I...don't know what's wrong with me. I just keep getting these really vivid dreams... *horrible* dreams about a lot of men in robes and Edward Kelley...you know, my apparent ancestor, is always in them...calling to me..." a wracking sob escaped from his mouth and he collapsed back onto the bed, exhausted.

Irene and Kelly looked at one another, a puzzled expression on both their faces. Irene shook her head and said. "Well I think you need to see a doctor...get some help? You're in a terrible state and you're making us nervous wrecks seeing you like this. I don't know how much more we can take!"

Dan rubbed a hand across his face, propped himself up on one elbow, and looked at his wife.

"Okay...you're right. I'll get it sorted..." he said, before collapsing back onto his pillows as his wife and daughter turned silently and left his room.

Two weeks later, and Dan still hadn't been to seek help.

The Scryer

His wife was staying at her sister's house in Kent and Kelly meanwhile had left in a teenage huff and gone to stay with friends back on the estate in south London leaving their respective husband/father to his own devices. Irene said that she would return if or when Dan finally made the effort to get himself sorted out.

And who could blame her?

Dan was now a shadow of his former self. He had lost over a stone and a half in weight and now looked sallow skinned and gaunt. He was never one to take a pride in his appearance, but he looked unkempt, dirty and unshaven, his hair greasy and unruly.

He also had a haunted look about him, his eyes red and always darting from side to side as though he could hear or see things which no one else could.

He had been on his own like this for a week, when the doorbell began to ring persistently, giving him no alternative but to either rip the thing off the wall or answer it.

He chose the latter of the options and was surprised to see the three elderly solicitors waiting patiently on his ample doorstep. Behind them, he could see several expensive cars parked around the circle of his driveway.

Oddly, although he was on the surface surprised to see these callers, he had somehow been expecting a further visit.

He opened the double oak doors wide and ushered the solicitors into the hallway, and couldn't help but notice how they stared at his appearance.

"Daniel…" began Michell Pink, "You look *dreadful*! Is everything alright?"

Dan smiled sardonically at Pink. "Does is *look* like everything is alright? Well…does it? I haven't slept for days…every time I *do* manage to doze off, I see *him!*" He was visibly shaking, and suddenly slumped down into one of the hall chairs as though the very life had been drained from his body.

Pink put a gnarled old hand on the younger man's shoulder.

"That is why we have come, Daniel. We…the rest of the coven and ourselves, have felt the call to come here and help you if we can."

Dan sat bolt upright in the chair and stared from one solicitor to the other.

"*Help* me? "Felt the call"? What the fuck are you talking about?! It's because of *you* – " and he pointed to each man in turn " – that I'm in this mess! I was fine before I heard from you lot and came to live in this …this shit hole!"

Mitchell Pink took a step back, unsettled by the sudden outburst.

Alistair Plunkett spoke next.

"We are aware that we have deceived you somewhat, Mr. Kelly…"he began.

"*"Deceived"* me!? I should bloody well say you've deceived me! You've led me into something that's ruined my life! This …this *business* is killing me!"

Plunkett was unruffled and continued. "However…and I am sincere when I say this, we *are* here to assist you in any way we can. I can only imagine what you have been experiencing over the last few weeks, but we know much about such things, having studied what is now laughingly referred to as 'The Black Arts' for many years between us. To put it bluntly, Mr. Kelly, we are your only hope…"

Dan ran his dirty fingers through his equally dirty

The Scryer

hair and smiled mirthlessly at Alistair Plunkett.

"Well...all I can say is, if you lot are my only hope, then I am well and truly fucked!"

The coven of thirteen men, including Dan, were assembled down in the cellar.

It was almost exactly as Dan had been dreaming over the weeks; all the men were dressed in black, hooded gowns with no one's – not even the three elderly solicitors – faces shown, so he had no notion as to who was who. Dan himself was also wearing one of the gowns which had been supplied by Gordon Wareham and he was seated, just as in the dreams, at a table (this was the only difference to the altar in his nightmares) with the Scrying mirror placed before him.

He felt strange. He had no recollection of coming down into the cellar, nor of the other twelve men joining him, or him getting changed into his donated robes, but another part of him seemed to know and understand *why* he was there and *what* was required of him. Yet another portion of his brain told him that this must be another of his hideous dreams. The line between reality and insanity was becoming increasingly blurred.

Then, the chanting began, the same words, or so they sounded, as the chanting in his nightmares. The rest of the coven were surrounding him forming a perfect circle, and they chanted as he sat at the table with the Scrying mirror set before him.

Was this another nightmare? *Could* this be reality?

As the chanting reached a crescendo, the Scrying mirror took on the now familiar misty appearance upon its surface and he was horribly aware that a face was appearing from the hazy depths. Dan tried to avert his gaze, but some force kept him focused on the mirror, unable to move or so much as even close his eyes or blink.

Then, a voice, an ancient, deep, booming voice filled the room, followed by a terrifying, maniacal laughter which reverberated through the entire cellar, echoing from the stone pillars and arched ceiling, filling his brain with the hideous sound until he felt his head might explode.

The chanting immediately stopped as soon as the laughter started, the hooded figures looking at one another anxiously, uncertainty clearly visible in their body language, as they slowly edged away from the desk and the Scrying mirror.

"DANIEL....DANIEL KELLEY..." said the voice from the mirror. The voice of Edward Kelley. The voice of a man supposed dead these last four hundred or so years.

The coven were now cowering in a corner of the vast cellar, congregated beneath one of the large stone arches.

Dan could only stare at the face in the mirror, the face which stared back at him, with deep black eyes and a terrifying expression. The face of a long dead yet not dead relative who had discovered the secrets of the ages, the mysteries of life after death.

"DANIEL KELLEY..THESE MEN ARE FOOLS! THEY SEEK TO USE YOU AND YOUR INHERITED POWER FOR THEIR OWN GAIN, TO ENHANCE THEIR PUNY LIVES AND TO RULE OVER OTHERS . BUT THEY ARE UNWORTHY DOGS!"

As the voice boomed around the stone walls, the coven whimpered like whipped curs as they shivered in

The Scryer

their terror, the terror of what they had now unleashed upon themselves. First one, then each and every one of them knelt on the hard cellar floor, heads bowed in supine surrender.

"LOOK AT THEM, DANIEL, ARE THEY NOT THE MOST UNWORTHY OF MEN?" and Dan did indeed look at the once powerful men as they wailed and hugged one another in their terror.

Slowly, the Scrying mirror began to glow with a faint yellow light, which gradually grew in intensity until it was blindingly white, filling the immense cellar with its brightness. Then, a shape moved from the mirror, the shape of a head at first, then shoulders, torso. Within the space of a minute, the person of Edward Kelley, Scryer to Doctor John Dee, alchemist and necromancer, stood in the room beside his only living relative.

Kelley extended his arms wide.

"Come to me, Daniel. Let us unite!" and as Dan stepped forward, as though in a deep state of trance, the two men seemed to merge into one, Edward Kelley absorbing the life force and substance of his distant relation, so that eventually only one man remained.

The ancient, now re-born Scryer turned back to the still glowing Scrying mirror and spoke.

"You see, my Lords? *This* is how it is done, as I have vowed to you through the years. Please, come forth and help yourself to a life renewed through these cowering curs!"

As the Scrying mirror glowed brightly once more, and the would-be necromancers finally found the courage to try and make a desperate break for life and freedom, they were overwhelmed by a far older and much more experienced band of twelve men who were truly versed in the black arts.

When finally, the screaming had abated, Edward Kelley addressed his faithful followers.

"We are come, my Lords, to a new world! Look ye not at the tired old bodies which some of you now inhabit, for there will be more suitable persons for us all. Whenever or whoever we so choose. This is the beginning, a *new* beginning for each and everyone of us. A beginning without end, my Lords!"

As a mighty cheer echoed around the cellar, the door at the top of the stairs opened.

"Dad, are you down there? Hope you don't mind, but I've brought a few mates back with me…"

"Ah…fresh meat, so soon!" whispered Edward Kelley, as he made his way up the stone stairs.

Guardian Devil

Guardian Devil

Stuart Young

"Enlighten me, yeah? What are we doing here?"

Becky considered the question carefully before replying. "Well, personally I suppose I'm trying to do some good and come to terms with my place in the world. To, if it's not too much of a cliché, give my life meaning."

"Nah, I mean what we doing *here*, in this dump."

"Oh, I think that was down to some of Devereux's clients. They like this sort of thing."

Becky glanced over at Sajid. He obviously felt uncomfortable in the strip club with its pounding music, flashing lights and nubile flesh. His religion forbade him from drinking any alcohol and every time his brown eyes ventured in the direction of the naked girls cavorting about on the various podiums he looked as if he would die of shock. Not that Becky blamed him. After seeing what one of the girls was doing Becky wasn't sure if she could ever bring herself to eat cucumber again.

She downed a quick swig of gin and tonic to steady her nerves and hide her discomfort. Becky liked to think she was fairly open-minded but some of the acts she had witnessed since arriving at the club would make the Marquis de Sade blush.

Averting her eyes from the chains and PVC and what looked like an industrial power tool she reminded herself that it was all for a good cause. The contacts she made here would supply the funding for a shelter for abused women she wanted to set up in Cable Street.

She knew Sajid had similar reasons for enduring this torture. As the limo drove them from Devereux's office to the strip club Sajid had told her about his plans for a drug rehab centre for local youths. His words had sounded strong and noble, his features dignified. Now he looked like he just wanted to hide.

At least there wasn't a crowd. The club had been booked as a private function; it was just them, Devereux and the three entrepreneurs they wanted to fund their respective projects. And of course the three dancers. No one else, not even bar staff. As far as drinks were concerned it was strictly help yourself.

She leaned over to Sajid. "I know it can't be easy for you coming here, what with you being a Hindu – "

Sajid's eyebrows jerked upwards. "I'm a Muslim."

"Oh." She felt her cheeks burn; she hoped the flashing lights would disguise it. "I just assumed, you know, with your beard ..."

Sajid shrugged, his own caramel skin dappled with red and green from the lights. "I'm Bengali; some of us are Hindi, but lots of us are Muslim. Either way, plenty of people happy to give us a kicking, innit? When I was a kid people even gave me a beating 'cos they thought I was Jewish."

"It's the nose that does it." Becky gestured to the large knot of bone and cartilage that dominated Sajid's face and then to her own inelegant proboscis.

Sajid grinned. "Mine was normal sized until some geezer gave me cosmetic surgery with a baseball bat. Didn't happen more than once though."

"People started to respect multiculturalism?"

"Nah. I learned to fight dirty." Just for a moment a little swagger came into Sajid's demeanour, a hint of braggadocio, but then his eyes filled with shame and he fingered his glass of mineral water nervously.

Becky wondered at his timidity. She rather liked the idea of narrow-minded bigots getting what they deserved. On the way here she had marvelled yet again at the mural depicting The Battle of Cable Street where the Jewish community of nineteen thirties London stood up to Oswald Mosley's Blackshirts. The mural had always been a symbol of inspiration for her ever since she was a child, and she knew many in the Muslim community felt the same way. They may not have been present for the showdown but it inspired them to know that there were those in Britain who would never bow to fascism, even when it was home-grown. She would have to point it out to Sajid after they finally managed to escape the strip club.

Of course, she realised, Sajid probably already knew all this as he lived in the area. A self-deprecating smile touched her lips; sometimes she took her do-gooder role too seriously, blinding her to basic realities. She really should know better by now.

Looking up she saw their host, Miles Devereux, approaching their table with a tray of fresh drinks. A tall handsome man in his early sixties Devereux held his slim body in an erect posture that spoke of vigour and determination, belying the strands of silver that filigreed his black hair. Reaching their table he flashed his straight white teeth in an apologetic smile. "I trust the entertainment is not *too* distasteful?"

Becky pulled a face. "This place makes Caligula look like a prude."

"It is a tad on the vulgar side." Devereux nodded to Sajid. "Ravi was asking after you. He thought you might join him and the others."

Becky looked over at the other table where the millionaires cavorted with the dancers. Alex Carruthers, shy until he had downed a few drinks; now he leered unattractively as he stuttered out lewd instructions to the dancers. Millicent Hoyle-Beckwith, an aging It girl, face drawn tight by too much cocaine and cosmetic surgery; a strong sneeze and her reconstructed septum would end up in her drink. Ravi Dhawan, barely five feet tall but with a wallet so thick it stood taller than he did. Millicent groped the dancers' breasts enthusiastically, tweaking nipples viciously, but Becky wasn't sure if she actually possessed Sapphic tendencies or if she was just doing this to excite the boys – or perhaps she just enjoyed inflicting pain. Ravi meanwhile used a fencing foil to stab one of the dancers in the buttocks. At first Becky assumed the foil was blunt but then she saw red spots forming, weeping across white flesh. Shivering in disgust Becky realised this wasn't just a strip club, it was also S&M.

Sajid didn't exactly look thrilled at the idea of spending time with the three lecherous millionaires but Becky knew he needed the money. Sighing, he made his way over.

Becky felt sympathy for him but wasn't exactly sorry to see him go. She was glad to have Devereux to herself. Despite his age he was a very attractive man and she often found herself fantasising about him peeling off her clothes, his confidence and piercing green eyes silencing her protestations as he proceeded to ravish her.

Devereux sipped from his brandy snifter – Delamain or La Fontaine de La Pouyade or some other cognac Becky had never heard of until he told her about it – and uttered a small appreciative murmur. "Fascinating history to this part of London. Did you know the Swedish mystic Emanuel Swedenborg lived just off Cable Street? Fellow swore that he conversed with angels. Also had some rather peculiar views on harlots and how they related to spirituality as I recall."

As Sajid sat down with the others, far enough away to be out of earshot, Devereux turned to Becky, his urbane manner evaporating, his face becoming tense, anxious. "I'm sorry, I've made the most terrible mistake."

"About Swedenborg?"

"About bringing you here. I was uncomfortable with the idea when I thought it was merely a night of debauchery, but now I realise it is something far worse."

Becky's eyes widened in horror. "Oh God. Don't tell me there's going to be karaoke."

"I'm serious. We are in grave danger. These people are Satanists."

Becky giggled. Sometimes Devereux could be so old-fashioned. "Look, I know that last song they played was heavy metal but that doesn't mean – "

Devereux cut her off sharply. "Look at the nipple piercings on that dancer."

Sipping her gin and tonic Becky glanced over. The piercings were inverted crucifixes.

"That doesn't prove anything. Lots of people use fashion accessories based on iconography they don't believe in."

"Perhaps. But that symbol on the wall behind us, the configuration of ten spheres connected by a network of pathways – looks rather like an Art Deco pantograph – is the Qabalistic Tree of Life. Except I think that in this case it represents the Tree of Death. And the letters on the floor tiling are from *The Book of Abramelin*." He tapped his finger on the round tray he had brought over, indicating the circular symbol with logos engraved upon it. "More worryingly, this is the Seal of Lucifer."

"So? Magic is a pretty common lifestyle choice in some circles. It's probably less creepy than this S&M stuff. I mean, it's not as if they're offering up some kind of sacrifice or anything."

Devereux's face fell. "Um, actually ..."

"Seriously? You really think they're going to slaughter a goat or something? That would violate all kinds of health and safety regulations. Plus, the RSPCA wouldn't be too pleased."

"It won't be a goat." Devereux placed his hand on hers; his touch was firm, his skin warm. "The post-mortem of Elizabeth Stride, one of Jack the Ripper's victims, was held near here in the vestry of the St George in the East church. Another of his victims, Mary Kelly, lived just off St George in the East at the crossroads between Cable Street and Ratcliff Highway. George Chapman, the Polish serial wife poisoner who was a suspect in the Ripper case had a barbershop in Cable Street. Maltese prostitutes used to frequent this area; the metal ankle chains denoting their price; gold the most expensive, silver the next. Women do not live well in Cable Street."

Devereux stared at Becky, his green eyes burrowing into hers. His voice took on that commanding tone that always made her feel about to swoon. "We need to get you out of here."

"That's very gallant of you but no, this is crazy. No one is planning to sacrifice me."

"I don't think you should take that chance. There are too many unsettling coincidences at work here. And that's before I found out about Sajid."

"What about Sajid?"

"When I was talking to Ravi and the others just now it came to light that Sajid is a pimp, running under-aged prostitutes."

Becky tried to speak but the words wouldn't come.

Devereux nodded sadly. "It's true." He passed her his smartphone; discreetly so that the others wouldn't notice. The screen showed a news article from five years ago detailing the arrest of a local pimp and drug dealer. The photo was of Sajid. Younger, clean-shaven, with a bitter anger burning in his eyes, but unmistakably Sajid.

A cold rage descended upon Becky. She had liked Sajid, had felt sorry for him, and all the time he was hiding this. A criminal. A pimp. A trafficker not just in women but in girls, too young and helpless to protect themselves.

The worst kind of man she could imagine.

Pushing herself up from the table she marched towards Sajid, her face tight, rigid. Sajid looked up at her approach, confused. He barely had time to open his mouth before she thrust Devereux's smartphone at him.

"Explain."

The word hit harder than a fist, a bullet, an atom bomb. All the air seemed to leave the room, leaving something that filled the lungs, kept the body functioning, but offered no real sustenance, nothing that let a person know that they were alive. Just a stale miasma of sweat and desperation masquerading as oxygen.

Sajid dropped his eyes to his mineral water as he mumbled a reply. "I don't do that no more."

"That's not what your pals told Devereux."

A frown creased Sajid's face then he jumped up, indignant, gesturing to Ravi and the others. "These ain't my friends."

Ravi looked hurt. "That's no way to convince us to fund your project."

He punched Sajid hard in the stomach. As Sajid doubled over, gasping in pain, Ravi pinned him to the table, facedown. Ravi grinned up at Becky. "He is right though. We aren't his friends."

Millicent stood and advanced menacingly towards Becky. "And we're not yours either."

Becky spun round to Devereux, looking for help. Instead he blocked her path and flashed her a roguish grin. "I told you that you needed to get out of here."

"I-I don't understand."

"It's really quite simple. We're black magicians, followers of the Left Hand Path. Seekers of enlightenment into the great mysteries. Unfortunately my path is guarded by the demon Samael. I am not powerful enough to defeat him and so I need a way to outwit him."

Devereux sipped his cognac. "Samael is host to the four angels of sacred prostitution. Using the appropriate rituals I can distract him long enough for my Holy Guardian Angel to reach enlightenment."

"Holy Guardian Angel?"

"My inner spirit. Everyone has one. A fact I'm going to use to my advantage. By combining the Holy Guardian Angels of the dancers with rituals associated with the four angels of sacred prostitution I can distract Samael long enough to get past him."

Becky squinted at the dancers. Ethereal figures floated above them, celestial versions of themselves, without the hard faces and dead eyes, full of grace and splendour. Then celestial versions of Ravi, Alex and Millicent swam into view; fanged, with glowing crimson eyes and all of them, even Millicent, possessing enormous scaly phalluses. Pouncing upon the glowing dancers they proceeded to rape them.

Becky cringed, appalled by the sight, horrified by the silent screams of the dancers. The figures faded from view and the dancers continued their soulless bump and grind up on their podiums. But now Becky could see the tears running down their cheeks.

She struggled to find her voice, a small frightened thing cowering deep inside her. "You said there were four angels of sacred prostitution. There are only three dancers."

"Well observed, my dear." Devereux nodded to Millicent who walked over to a side door, opened it, and led a tiny figure in by the hand.

A little girl.

Small, delicate; dressed in pyjamas and clutching a teddy bear. She didn't look scared; her smooth round face was impassive, her feet shuffled aimlessly. The pupils of her large blue eyes were so dilated that her eyes were almost totally black. Drugged.

"This is Lucy." Devereux smiled. "She's the fourth angel. Unless there are any other volunteers?"

Everyone looked at Becky. Devereux and his cronies; grinning and leering. Sajid, wincing in pain, his arm still forced up behind his back. Even the dancers with their soulless eyes which somehow still leaked tears. The only person who didn't look at Becky was Lucy. She just gazed into empty space with her wide drugged up eyes.

Becky trembled. She couldn't take Lucy's place. She couldn't cope with what the dancers were experiencing. It would destroy her. Let Devereux take Lucy instead. Maybe then he would let Becky go and she could flee into the night and lose herself in drink and drugs and whatever else it would take to make her forget all this.

Or maybe Devereux would make her watch.

Becky took a deep breath. Deep enough to strangle the scream that built within her. So deep that when she finally spoke her voice was unnaturally calm.

"I'll do it."

*

Sajid's shoulder hurt like hell. Bones ground together, muscles and tendons twisted into a knot of agony. Ravi slamming his head against the table hadn't helped. His vision had exploded, a firework display of five-pointed stars. It was beautiful. Then his head cleared -- the only five points he saw belonged to the pentagram Alex was painting on the floor.

No, not a pentagram. A triangle.

Tray lying next to Sajid's head had symbols on it too. Circles; squiggles inside them like graffiti tags. The tray was round too; circles within circles. Trays on the other tables had the same symbols.

Little girl had a tray, smaller, more like a plate. Silver. Laid out in front of her; stared at it with doped up eyes.

Sajid struggled to get up; Ravi kept him pinned to the

table. Fucking embarrassing being taken down by this midget. Never would've happened back in the day. Back then Sajid would've left him a broken mess on the floor.

But that was before prison. Before finding Allah. Before Sajid realised what scum he had been.

He wasn't the scum now. That was that Devereux geezer, pretending to be all high and mighty but really just a piece of shit that had learned to walk and talk and wear a suit.

The suit had been ditched for a set of robes. Showing his true colours. Still talked like he was off *Downton fucking Abbey* though.

Music switched off. Lights too. Candles instead, scented ones, circles of them.

Devereux to Becky: "I assure you that it'll be much easier if you don't struggle while Millicent helps you disrobe."

Becky stood still while Millicent pulled down Becky's skirt, unbuttoned her blouse. Becky's bra and knickers didn't match colours, not that it mattered, they didn't stay on long. One of Becky's hands covered her tits, the other her bush, just for a split second, then her face went all 'Fuck you' and she let her hands hang by her sides.

Sajid watched her, mesmerised.

A bit bigger than the dancers, a little roll of flab developing around her belly. Bush neat but visible, not waxed or shaved into wispy nothingness. And the tits, slight sag as gravity fondled them, no silicone to hold them up.

Long time since Sajid saw a real woman. His dick twitched. Just a little. Still, he hated himself for it.

Thought he was past that; reacting to women like

they were meat. Just wanted a wife. Treat her right, with respect like it said in the *Qur'an*, not with that mediaeval bullshit some people read into it.

Millicent laid Becky down upon the podium. Devereux stood over her. "I'm glad you chose to do this, Becky. Although I would have gone through with the ritual with Lucy if necessary I would have found it rather discomforting. My tastes are not as exotic as some of Sajid's clients."

"I don't do that shit no more!"

Devereux cocked an eyebrow to Ravi. "If he speaks again, feel free to remove his tongue."

Sajid shut up.

Standing over Becky Devereux began to chant, Latin or some language that Sajid didn't recognise. Misshapen half-words choked off before they even got started; harsh syllables strangled at birth. Sounded like a ventriloquist doing their act while gargling battery acid.

Switched to English:

"Thee I invoke, the Bornless One.

Thee, that didst create the Earth and the Heavens.

Thee that didst create the Night and the Day.

Thee, that didst create the darkness and the light."

The chant ended. Devereux looked down at Becky.

He took off his robe.

*

Under normal circumstances Becky might have laughed. She might have shown sympathy. Regardless, she would have been disappointed. But here, now, she didn't know what she felt.

Devereux had the tiniest penis she had ever seen.

Barely three inches long as it jutted out above his equally miniscule scrotum. Even shaving his pubic hair hadn't helped; his puny erection looked pathetic.

If anyone else thought likewise they said nothing, although Becky got the impression that Devereux's followers were making a point of not looking below his waist. She wished they would, that they would laugh and point and humiliate Devereux to the point where he couldn't go through with this.

But he *was* going to go through with it.

Becky bit her lip, trying to cut off her emotions. This was only happening to her body, she could treat it as an illness (a terrible, terrible illness) which, no matter how unpleasant, could be endured, leaving her no worse than before. Devereux couldn't touch her mind, her soul. (But he intended to defile her Holy Guardian Angel, wasn't that part of her soul?). Her body was strong. (Shit, he's not going to wear a condom.) Her body could endure anything. (Oh God, don't let him have any diseases.)

Devereux stepped closer to her, smiling. Slowly, his genitals metamorphosed into a scorpion.

His testicles became claws, snapping away like angry castanets. A short, scaly body connected them to his penis, now transformed into the scorpion's tail, a drop of venom beading around the stinger.

The venom dripped onto Becky's labia.

It burned. Like poison, like acid, like the fires of hell itself. She screamed but the venom burned so fiercely that it caused her voice to evaporate, leaving only anguished silence.

Devereux entered her.

She could smell his cologne mixing with the aroma of her burned flesh. She could see the tracery of fine lines that mapped his tanned face, twisting and warping as his expression contorted with obscene joy. She could feel the weight of him crushing her. But mostly she could feel the pain.

The scorpion's claws nipped at her flesh, the tail writhed inside her, tearing, slicing.

Everything changed colour, the world outlined in sky blue. Devereux's cologne turned to sandalwood. The club faded away. She saw a figure watching her, a woman, so beautiful that the stars themselves paled. A pair of angels flew down to the woman, enraptured by her beauty. They made love to her and when they had finished her belly was round with child. Opening her legs she spewed forth a host of demons.

Becky felt as though she were engaged in childbirth herself, except that the children were being forced up inside her, crowding her womb. The pain was unbearable.

Tears rolled down her cheeks.

Gradually the pain receded, colours shifted, sky blue became purple. Around her swam images of Devereux ravishing her; the fantasies she had savoured of him stripping away her clothes and inhibitions, taking her forcefully and passionately as her cries of distress turned to moans of pleasure. Him bending her over her office desk, scattering pens and files. Devereux as a brooding vampire, his fangs sending her into paroxysms of ecstasy as they nibbled her clitoris. In the bunk of his pirate ship, him grinning roguishly as he tore open her bodice. Against the wall of his castle dungeon, her in chains, his armour cold and metallic, the only thing warm about him his hot, thrusting cock. Romanticised rape, sexual assault by Mills and Boon.

The reality was somewhat different. Squalid,

terrifying, dehumanising.

She tried to switch off the images, this wasn't how she had intended to block out the horror of the rape, but they continued to swim around her. A suspicion dawned; somehow Devereux was plucking them from the depths of her subconscious, making his violation of her complete.

More images appeared. Not her sanitised fantasises; these belonged to Devereux.

Devereux as a dashing secret agent, shackled to the wall as Becky interrogated him; she slapped him across the face then slid down and unzipped his trousers, taking him in her mouth, bringing him to the brink of climax before stepping back, refusing to go any further unless he revealed the details of his mission.

Devereux asleep in his bed, Becky flying in through the window to sit astride him, a naked succubus riding him in his sleep: he moaned in pleasure as she stole his seed.

Devereux as a Roman slave, Becky as his mistress, smiling lasciviously as she divested him of loincloth and coaxed life into his frightened penis; she could fuck him or have him executed as the whim took her, his life depended on his ability to pleasure her.

Another figure stood watching Becky. Another woman, with black skin; blacker than coal, blacker than ebony, as though the night had taken on human form. Becky cried out for help but the woman just smiled; lips curling, her teeth sharp and jutting. In the distance Becky saw an elderly man in powdered wig, waistcoat and breeches, surrounded by erotic angels, his face a picture of confusion and delight.

Becky frowned. These last images had nothing to do

with the roles she and Devereux had conjured for each other.

The images dwindled. Everything took on an orange tinge.

She squirmed beneath Devereux's body. He didn't seem to even be aware of her anymore, he kept thrusting away mechanically, his face blank as though engaged in calculating complex mathematical equations. Hoping to use Devereux's distraction against him Becky arched her back, attempting to lever him off of her. As soon as she tried the scorpion's claws clamped onto her flesh, threatening to tear muscles and arteries if dislodged.

But this wasn't her real body. This was some kind of astral projection or a vision from her subconscious. Except she was sure the pain she felt was what her physical body had experienced back on earth.

Looking around she saw a giant chessboard far below her. Each square contained a letter, as had the tiled floor in the S&M club. There was a pattern to the letters, groups of them spelled out the same two words, Milon and Ogari, forming a square grid as the words repeated themselves horizontally and vertically; an occult wordsearch puzzle.

Figures stood upon the chessboard; the white army represented by naked, scared, bedraggled humans; the black army by naked zombies. A black pawn shuffled forward and took the white king, raping him to death with savage glee. The king faded to nothingness while the pawn grew in stature, dwarfing the other pieces. At the same time its rotting penis fell away to reveal a tooth-studded vagina; the pawn had become a queen.

At the far side of the board stood a throne carved from bones and skulls and lashed together with tendons.

On the throne sat a horned figure, with twelve wings sprouting from his back. The two women Becky had seen earlier draped themselves across him, along with two other females who Becky did not recognise. The horned figure gestured with his left hand and the figures on the board moved.

A hum throbbed across the landscape. Low, menacing; it vibrated through Becky's body, leaving nausea in its wake. Angry high-pitched screeches skewered the hum, stabbing at it in a manic counterpoint, with no concern for rhythm or tempo.

Becky and Devereux drifted away from the chessboard and the freakishly disturbing sounds.

Becky tried again to shut off her emotions, to remember that in reality the only violation was of her body, not of her mind, but the memory of the images she had witnessed mocked her attempts. The scars from this would cut much deeper than the merely physical.

Devereux still worked within her. The rape was lasting an eternity. Time moved at a different rate here.

A garden of luscious greenery sprang up around Becky and Devereux. Vines wrapped around Becky, their embrace impossible to break. Their touch did not match their beauty; they were some kind of cross between stinging nettles and a Venus flytrap; green jaws left burning red welts. Devereux appeared untroubled by them, if anything they only increased his ardour. Becky writhed frantically; still she could not break free. As she struggled she became more enraged.

Becky loathed Devereux for doing this to her. Hated Sajid for being a pimp (even if he had looked genuinely distressed by the proceedings; maybe he really had given all that up.) Despised herself for being so stupid.

The vines released their hold and drooped back to the ground; swollen, sluggish, like a snake that had just consumed a large meal.

Becky floated away from the garden. Slowly, by some strange unfathomable alchemy, her anger transformed to gold. Hate, fear and anger became love and happiness, glistening brightly like the golden mountain that had materialised around her.

She was standing now. Devereux had gone. It was just her and this wonderful sense of joy and completion.

And the young man who stood before her.

He was beautiful. Blue eyes, golden curls, lean sculpted muscles and a smile that could induce orgasms. His white robe rippled in the warm breeze as he spoke. "Hello, Becky. I'm your inner spirit. Your Holy Guardian Angel."

Becky blinked. "Shouldn't you be female?"

"A Holy Guardian Angel is not necessarily of the same gender as its human host. Besides, it makes sense that I would be male. Women need a man to protect them."

Becky frowned slightly. Her inner spirit was a male chauvinist? "Just tell me what's going on. Where's Devereux?"

"With his own Holy Guardian Angel, licking his wounds at how easily I defeated him."

"So he's gone? I'm safe?"

"For the moment. He was using the ritual to ascend the Qabalistic Tree of Life, moving towards transcendence. The Tree is a glyph, tracing a map of both human consciousness and the universe. Each Sephiroth, or sphere, is a different realm of consciousness and of reality. Now that his spiritual union with you has been severed your path back to earth will be blocked. You no longer represent one of the four angels of sacred prostitution; you will not be able to pass Samael."

"Who?"

"The Angel of Death. The Lord of the Left Hand Path."

Becky stared at him in confusion.

Her Holy Guardian Angel sighed. "The gentleman with the horns and the chessboard."

"Wait, wasn't he the one blocking Devereux's path to enlightenment? If we've got past him doesn't that mean he's already enlightened? Does that mean *I'm* enlightened? Because frankly I'm confused as hell."

"You are currently in the Sephiroth of Tipareth. Enlightenment comes in the highest Sephiroth, Kether. You have a long way to go if you want to beat Devereux there."

"Why do I need to beat him? Let him become enlightened, maybe then the bastard'll stop raping people."

"You need to reach Kether to become enlightened so that you can get past Samael and return to earth. Until then you are no match for Devereux."

The angel's words made sense, as much as anything did make sense in this magical madhouse, but somehow Becky remained unconvinced. There was something about the angel's demeanour, a hint of condescension that teetered on the brink of full-blown arrogance, that unsettled her.

Something else felt wrong, something vitally important, but she couldn't quite place it. Then she realised.

She wasn't upset.

Back on earth she was being raped, defiled, violated. Yet apart from a faint nagging suspicion, she felt fine. Better than fine. She felt *happy*.

Something, or someone, was messing with her emotions, trying to control her reaction to events.

A faint clicking sound came from the angel's fingers as they brushed together. It sounded like claws. Becky frowned; the clicking came from the angel's left hand. Devereux had said he and his cronies had followed the Left Hand Path.

She started to back away.

The angel smiled. His left hand transformed into a scorpion.

She wondered if she had left it too late to run. "You're not my Holy Guardian Angel."

"No, he's not."

Becky turned to see a hooded figure standing behind her. "*I* am."

*

The handcuffs bit into Sajid's wrists. Even the fluffy pink covering didn't stop them pinching his skin.

Ravi glared at Alex. "Are these the best handcuffs you could get?"

Alex blushed. "T-t-t-they're the ones my wife and I always use for r-r-r-role-play."

Didn't matter how gay-looking the cuffs were, Sajid couldn't break them. So he couldn't do a fucking thing when Ravi and the others started to undress him.

Ravi undid his shoelaces; Alex unbuckled his belt; Millicent unravelled his tie. He struggled; they just shoved him down into a chair so Ravi could slide off his shoes.

Sajid stared around, frantic; no one there to help him. The dancers were out of it; drugs – rocks or brown or something – the gear he used to keep in lots all over Banglatown. Little kid was no help either; eyes blank, hugging the teddy bear to the logo on her pyjamas – 'Unwrap Me.' Just a baby, shouldn't have shit like that on her clothes.

Ravi had eased off Sajid's jacket before snapping on the cuffs. Now he went to work on his shirt, unbuttoning it slowly, running his hands over Sajid's body. Skin soft, smooth; plastic feel to it. Like being fondled by a sex doll. Sajid flinched: "Get off me, you queer!"

Ravi smiled; licked his lips. "Now, now. We've got a ritual to perform."

Sajid's eyes bulged, staring at where Devereux was fucking Becky on the stage. Ravi nodded. "That's right. *That* kind of ritual."

Sajid exploded. Feet lashed out, hands shoved; mouth yelled, shouted, *screamed*. Fell off the chair, scraped skin off his knees. Before he could stand Ravi was over him, burying his fist. Only in his kidney, thank Allah, but it still hurt like fuck.

Alex helped drag him to his feet. "G-g-go easy on him. This is only r-r-r-role-play."

"Of course it is." Ravi grinned at Alex. "He's loving every second of it."

Standing on tiptoe he kissed Sajid on the lips, tongue probing deep.

It felt like a slug in Sajid's mouth, twisting, writhing. Saliva filled his dry mouth, spilling over his lips, dribbling down his beard. He jerked his head away, retching.

"Don't hog all the fun." Millicent slid Sajid's trousers over his ankles then slipped her hands inside his boxers. Cock shrivelled at her touch; not what she was after anyway. She worked her hands round to his arse. "Ooh, nice and smooth. Just how I like them."

This wasn't right. They couldn't treat him like this. But then it wasn't right the way the girls Sajid used to pimp got treated either.

He hadn't planned getting into that shit. Started out just chillin' and rollin' with his posse; all "Yo, s'up, bruv? Got any brown?" That led to dealing, soon he was top shotta in this turf. Wasn't like drugs were anything new to Cable Street. Opium dens used to cover the place; back in the sixties hashish and mandrax were everywhere, white boys looking to get high or seek enlightenment from Sufi mystics, they got the one, didn't really care about the other.

But he couldn't be caught holding; any plots he couldn't give to his soldiers he hid with one of his girlfriends. Five O couldn't keep track of all his bitches; they couldn't touch him. Using women for one thing, might as well use them for another; running hos was a sideline, almost a hobby. But the punters got kinkier, offered more cash.

He was butt naked now; they had even torn his shirt to shreds to save time undoing the cuffs. The others were all naked too; Ravi and Alex ground their hard-ons against his hip and his thigh; his sphincter was too tight to let them in. Instead Millicent jammed her finger up there, wiggled it around. Felt like a tree trunk rammed inside him; a gnarled old oak come to life, horny for Sajid's arse. The worst thing was she wore a diamond ring; it slashed and tore and gouged, digging new tunnels with each savage twist.

Tears rolled down Sajid's cheeks.

Girls he sold cried too. The underage ones anyway. Barely old enough to bleed at one end and if they didn't do what he said they bled at the other. He felt bad about it, but what could he do? He was a businessman. Besides, he wasn't the only one to do this shit. Back in his parents' country underage girls were sold as Devadasi, slaves to Yellama, the goddess of fertility. Lose their cherry to one of the priests, become sanctified hos; being slave to Yellama supposed to bring good fortune, stop crop failure and all that shit. Brought good fortune to the parents; money the girls earned from fucking whoever bought them in auction went straight to mum and dad. Some people said Devadasi was disgusting, made it illegal. Others – PC anthropology types – said it was an important cultural and spiritual tradition.

And only about a century ago Victorian pervs were complaining that the English age of consent had been raised from twelve to thirteen. Even now some sickos were talking about lowering it back to that.

He wasn't the sicko. He wasn't the pervert. He had just done what he needed to do to survive.

That's what he told himself.

Millicent's voice in his ear, a singsong chant: "The four magical weapons: Disc."

She spanked Sajid's buttocks with a round serving tray.

"Sword."

Ravi poked Sajid's chest with the point of the foil, drawing blood.

"Wand."

Alex rapped him half-heartedly on the thigh with a candlestick.

Ravi, leering, thrusting his cock harder: "How do you like *my* magic wand?"

Gut heaved. Too disgusted to answer.

"Cup."

Grunting, Ravi dropped the foil, scooped a glass of scotch off a nearby table and poured it into Sajid's mouth. Sajid spluttered, desperate to avoid swallowing, to keep the fiery liquid from entering his stomach.

Hadn't touched alcohol since prison. Hadn't expected to end up there. One of his bitches grassed on him – "I warned you, Sajid! You can't treat me like this!" Shit, she'd had it easy, he hadn't even made her sell her pussy. Planned to visit her when he got out. Mess up her life, her face. But someone visited him instead.

Allah.

Ravi and Alex were grinding faster and faster, excited pants sounding in his ears. Millicent plunged fingers deep inside herself while twisting one finger inside of him. Moaning, she fell back, one digit smeared with shit and blood. A hot splash as Ravi squirted all over him. Then another as Alex did the same. Warm spunk slithered down his body.

This would never have happened before he found Allah. If the Somalis or the Poles or whoever-the-fuck-else had a problem Sajid and his soldiers would sort them out. Turf wars, stroppy punters, or just good old honky bashing, Sajid was there. Didn't matter if they were tooled up like the Poles, shooters didn't bother Sajid. Last time someone popped a cap at him he broke the fucker's arm with a crowbar.

But he wasn't that man no more.

Ravi poured the rest of the scotch into Sajid's mouth. "Was it good for you too?"

Sajid spat the scotch into Ravi's eyes.

Ravi staggered back, clutching at his burning eyeballs. Sajid lunged at Millicent with both hands, hitting her with the chain linking the handcuffs, breaking her jaw. The crunch of bone merged with the snap of cheap handcuff links. Her fake septum exploded from her nose, flew through the air, bounced off Sajid's cheek.

Hands free, Sajid spun round, glared at Alex. Shy, sensitive Alex; eyes wide, voice meek as he machine-gunned out an apology. "I-I-I thought this was r-r-r-role-play."

Sajid punched him in the throat. Slammed his head against the wall a few times to see which was tougher. The wall won.

Sajid turned back to finish off Ravi. Just in time for something sharp to pierce his arm, sending shards of pain jangling through his body.

Ravi clutched the fencing foil he had been dicking around with earlier. Smirking like he was fucking Zorro; the point of his blade driven right through Sajid's left biceps and into the wall, pinning him there.

Ravi's smirk widened. "'Curses! Foiled again!'"

*

The hooded figure glared at the blonde Holy Guardian Angel. "Hello, Devereux."

The angel smiled. "Actually, Devereux is my mortal name. In this form I much prefer Master."

"How about Deluded Fuckwit?"

"That does have a certain ring to it. Unfortunately

I've already ordered my personalised stationery."

The hooded figure nodded. It was clear from her voice that she was female, but that was all Becky could discern past the ankle-length grey robe; its voluminous cowl seemed to contain only shadows.

"You should walk away, Devereux. I have magicks that could melt you where you stand."

An elegant eyebrow arched in amusement. "I told you – my name is Master." Energy flashed from his fingertips, smashing the hooded figure to the ground. He turned to a quaking Becky, blew her a kiss, then vanished.

Becky helped the hooded figure to her feet. "Are you all right?"

"I'm fine. Come on, we have to keep moving if we want to beat him to Kether."

Becky didn't move. "That's what *he* said I should do. Why should I trust you?"

"Apart from me stopping Devereux get his grubby mitts on you?" The woman pulled back the hood, revealing her face. "This a good enough reason?"

Becky gasped. The woman was *her*.

Older, greyer, with a web of scars mixed in with her wrinkles, but still unmistakably her. Becky knew she should be repelled by the scars, the ancient ruin of her face, but she wasn't. Not here. Her face was beautiful.

Her older self grabbed Becky's arm, steered her onwards. "In some models of the Holy Guardian Angel the HGA is a future version of the person's self travelling back along the person's timeline to offer their past self help and advice. Understand?"

"I-I ..."

"Good. Call me Rebecca."

"So if you're my future self then that means I survive this?"

"I'm a version of you that *might* survive this. Nothing's certain."

That didn't exactly encourage Becky. Yet at the same time she found it strangely comforting. Rebecca was giving it to her straight, no lying like Devereux. Strange as it was to converse with her future self it also felt right.

If only that could do something about the feelings of being raped. Nausea hit her. Hard. She staggered along beside Rebecca, trying not to puke up whatever it was that astral bodies puke up.

The golden mountain faded, replaced by a power station, pumping out some kind of mystical electricity. The landscape turned red, a deep fiery crimson.

It didn't help Becky's mood.

"Next time you see Devereux don't talk. Just blast the fucker."

"That was a bluff. I don't have the power to take him in a fair fight."

"Then don't give him a fair fight."

Rebecca shot Becky an appraising look. "Sound strategy. But I'm not sure if it's a sound judgement. Is it coming from your head or your gut?"

"What?"

"Devereux's manipulated you, lied to you. Back on earth his physical body is raping you. So when you say not to give him a fair fight you're not just thinking about survival; you're talking about revenge."

Becky glared at her. "Are you saying I shouldn't?"

"I'm saying that might be exactly what Devereux wants you to do." Rebecca stopped walking. "When sorcerers enter into Knowledge and Conversation with the Holy Guardian Angel they have to make all demons swear allegiance to the sorcerer. Without that pact the demons get to have the sorcerer as a snack; usually it'll present as psychological problems – the demons acting as a personification of the sorcerer's fears and flaws – but right here, right now, the demons are real."

Rebecca looked at Becky. "Devereux made a pact with the demons. Did you?"

"No, I – "

Rebecca pointed downward. Becky could make out different realms below them, she guessed these were the Sephiroth she had already passed through. Within each one writhed hideous creatures. Demons. Some Becky recognised, some of them she had not even noticed whilst in those realms, but she realised with a shock that they had been there all along. The demons all glared upwards, hungering for her.

Stomach fluttering, she broke into a run.

Rebecca puffed along beside her. "What makes it worse is that each Sephiroth has a reverse side that homes demons called the Qliphoth. It means shells, husks. It also means harlots. Devereux wasn't using you and the other girls to distract Samael. He was using you to attract the Qliphoth."

Becky's hatred for Devereux burned even harder than her aching lungs. "Why?"

"I'm not sure. Different beings rule the Qliphotic counterparts to the regular Sephiroth – Samael instead of Michael, Thagirion instead of Raphael – I think he's trying to use their demonic energy to supercharge his ascent to Kether. Anyway, we have to get out of here before the ruler of this realm senses you."

A rider appeared in the distance. He had three heads

— that of a sheep, a bull and a man spitting fire. His steed had the body of a lion and the wings of a dragon.

Rebecca grimaced. "Too late. That's Asmodeus. Keep moving. He hasn't pinpointed us yet."

"Can you stop him?"

"Maybe if I had a fish heart and liver to throw on red-hot cinders. But I don't, so it's up to you."

"How the hell do *I* stop it?"

"You stay calm. Let go of your rage."

"I don't think I can."

Rebecca squeezed her hand. "You don't have to let go of it completely. Not yet. Just transform it, find a balance."

Easier said than done. Becky wanted to kill Devereux. Slowly. Shattering each bone in his body a dozen times before moving onto the next. But she couldn't do that if she were dead. Her hate couldn't be the thing that got her killed, it had to be the thing that kept her alive. She would survive so she could murder the bastard.

Asmodeus drew closer, a lance in his hand, a banner fluttering from its point. Behind him marched an army of demons, legion after legion stretching across the hellscape.

"He can feel your hate."

Becky took a deep breath. All right, she wouldn't murder Devereux, she would execute him. Not just in revenge for what he was doing to her but for what he had done to the dancers and what he had threatened to do to the little girl. His crimes couldn't go unpunished, his victims deserved some salve for their pain, a sense of rightness restored to the world. His death wouldn't be vengeance, it would be justice.

A sense of shame came over her that until now she had not thought of the dancers as victims. Although she instinctively felt pity for what Devereux and his cronies had done to them there was still a part of her that felt that given their profession they must accept danger and abuse as a potential by-product of their work. On some level they almost deserved it for choosing such a dubious career path. Now she realised that was faulty thinking on her part. No one *deserved* what had been done to those girls.

A tear came to her eye. It wasn't the first one she had shed since this all began, but it was the first that wasn't for herself.

Slowly, Asmodeus and his demon armies faded into nothingness. Becky and Rebecca slowed their pace until they stood doubled over, panting for breath.

Around them the world turned blue. A woman appeared, a beautiful giant, filling the heavens. She danced, her hips swaying in a hypnotic rhythm. Slowly, enticingly, she started to peel off her clothes.

Rebecca nodded towards the woman. "That's Ishtar. Goddess of Love."

"Does that mean we're safe?"

"She's also the Goddess of War. In terms of the Tree of Death she's linked to the Qliphoth."

"I'm confused. Are we on the Tree of Life or the Tree of Death?"

"I think we're on both."

"So we're not safe?"

"We won't be safe until we get you back to earth."

Becky nodded. Getting back to earth sounded good to her. The sooner she was free of this psychedelic hellhole the better.

About them Ishtar continued to shed her clothes until she stood naked. Her flawless flesh glowed as she continued her sinuous undulations.

Rebecca pointed to a seething mass of chaos that lay ahead. Galaxies twisted in upon themselves. Celestial vultures fed on the carcasses of dead solar systems. Entire realities were shredded beyond repair. A rainbow bridge led into the centre of the tumult before being swallowed by cosmic anarchy.

"We have to cross that."

Becky gulped. She would rather take her chances with the demons.

"We can't go back," said Rebecca. "We have to go forward. Crossing the Abyss is the only way to get you back to earth."

Becky frowned as a worrying thought struck her. "But when I get back to earth the real Devereux will be waiting for me. I'll be no better off."

"Don't worry. I have a plan."

"Are you going to teach me some sort of spell or hex to stop him?"

Rebecca shook her head. "Punch him in the throat."

Becky stared at her. "Are you crazy? He'll just go all Harry Potter on me. Even if I did knock him out I'd still have to deal with the Three Stooges."

"The situation on earth has changed. I can't sense the exact details but Devereux's lost his backup. The energy his acolytes were sending into the Tree has changed. Only one of them is still connected."

"Is that why Devereux legged it after he zapped you? I mean, I'm supposed to be integral to his plan but he didn't grab me when he had the chance."

"Maybe. I don't know his plans. I can't even make an

educated guess, the rituals he's using are such a mishmash. He's drawing on a combination of traditional spells, radical reinterpretations of classic rituals plus a bunch of stuff he appears to have made up himself. I have no idea if he's improvising this whole thing or if he planned it this way all along."

"Actually, my dear, it's a little of both."

They spun round to see Devereux smiling at them, his golden hair glinting in the lilac glow of the energies that raged within the Abyss. Before Becky or Rebecca could react he launched himself forward, wrapping his arms around them both and knocking them into the inferno.

Eddies of chaos tore at Becky, clawing at her soul. She screamed, the sound turning into the ringing of a bell, endless tintinnabulations of terror. She grabbed at Rebecca, clinging to her for support to get through this horror, this madness. Her fingers closed on nothingness; at her touch Rebecca transformed into strands of withered ivy then crumpled and vanished.

Becky was alone with Devereux in the heart of the maelstrom.

*

Blade twisted, tearing up skin and muscle. Squirming to get free just made it worse.

Ravi, laughing. "A bit late to go all *jihad*. The ritual's nearly finished. Now we just sit back and wait for the grand finale."

Jihad. Inner spiritual struggle. Every stupid fucker went for the other interpretation: death and violence.

Right now that was Sajid's interpretation too.

He lashed out with his foot, aiming to stomp his heel down on Ravi's knee. Ravi skipped aside, letting go of the sword.

Sajid grabbed the blade – didn't cut him, only the point was sharp – and tried to yank it free of his arm. Stuck fast. Stretched, shifted his grip to the hilt, tugged from a different angle. All he did was bend the blade, curving the hilt back towards him.

Ravi: mocking applause. "That's the spirit. Don't give up. You – "

Sajid let go the sword. Blade sprang back into place, whipping the hilt into Ravi's smug face. Blood mingled with his scowl, making him ugly. "You little shit!"

Ravi seized the sword again; twisted. Sajid screamed. "You think this is bad? This is just foreplay. There's something coming you won't believe."

In the background Millicent gagged; choking on her own tongue, French kissing herself to death. After a few seconds she lay still.

How long before Sajid joined her?

Arm felt like it had been torn apart. Sword kept him pinned in place.

On the way here Devereux told a story about a 19th century murderer who committed suicide and ended up buried in Cable Street with a stake through his heart. Suicide was a sin; stake would keep him pinned in his grave, stop his ghost tormenting the living.

Sajid's sins had been buried, but no stake, they came back. He had sinned again, had killed. Now he was being punished. Only way out was more killing, more sinning.

Sword carved up his arm some more. Ravi laughed. Fucking dwarf was getting off on this.

Candlestick to Sajid's right. If he could just reach it

he'd fuck up Ravi's face even more.

Ravi twisted the sword again. Enjoying the screams of pain too much to notice anything else.

Fingertips groped. Brushed metal. Seized it. Swung.

Everything counted on this. Saving the little girl, the dancers, Becky. Everything.

The candlestick missed.

The flame from the candle didn't. Kissed Ravi's cheek, igniting the scotch Sajid had spat in his face. Bastard's head went up in a sheet of flame. Ravi fell to the floor, screaming like a little bitch.

Sajid slotted the candlestick through the hilt, bent the blade again, levered on it – hard. Blade popped free in a spray of blood.

Wincing, Sajid flung the sword aside. It clattered against the floor.

Hefted the candlestick. Marched over to Ravi; rolling on the floor, batting at the flames like a crazy person.

Flames sputtered, died, leaving charred skin and the stink of burning meat.

Sajid dropped a knee on Ravi's chest; pinned him in place. Raised the candlestick high.

Metal hit bone. Once. Twice. Too many times to count. Bone cracked, shattered, splintered. Blood leaked out. Brains too.

All the time screaming: "How do you like *my* magic wand, fucker?"

Ravi's leg spasmed, trying to tap out a reply in Morse code. After a while it gave up.

Finally, exhausted, Sajid staggered to his feet. Little girl and the dancers still stared with vacant eyes. Devereux still thrust away on top of Becky. Bastard was too caught up in his magic fuckfest to know what was going on around him.

Sajid stumbled forward. Drag Devereux off of Becky, call Five O and then get the fuck out of here, never come back, never tell anyone what had been done to him.

Behind him – air pressure dropped, world twisted by words spoken in a voice that belonged in Hell: "Zazas, Zazas, Nasatanada Zazas."

The snap and crack of broken bones, the pop of bursting skin, the sucking sound of internal organs flipping inside out.

He turned. Eyes bulged; candlestick dropped from his hand.

Ravi's body stretched into a strange new shape. Extra limbs, three or four bloated new abdomens, half a dozen metallic wings.

Angry roar echoed around the club: "Who dares summon Choronzon?"

Oh fuck.

*

Myriads of broken reflections, spiralling in upon each other, distorting into chaotic incoherence. Images splinter, form dissolves. Drunk Picasso battling it out with stoned Escher and acidhead Pollock.

Colours scream. Scents beg for mercy.

Insane gods cackle dementedly as they wallow in their own divine excrement. Computers carved from the skulls of chimeras running on alchemical software written in eight dimensional trinary code. A dozen different Heavens shatter into a shower of celestial confetti.

Devereux clung to Becky. She squirmed in his grasp but couldn't shake him loose. Whatever this was, they would endure it together.

Except Devereux seemed unaffected by the turmoil. It was all directed at Becky.

Buffeted by spiritual tornadoes, existential hurricanes. Whirlwinds composed of her every doubt and fear, tearing at her, stripping away all that she was, leaving nothing but terror.

thought her first time would be romantic but it hurt so much as aaron pierced her hymen she wasn't enjoying it at all but when she said so aaron didn't care he turned into a giant spider each leg a hungry cock but she screamed no making him scuttle away so she was all alone and in europe on her gap year with her best friend angela sharing a hotel bed to save money then waking up to find angela kissing her groping at her angela's hands turning to crabs and lobsters scuttling all over her body becky telling angela she didn't feel that way about her angela crying then storming off so she was all alone and years from now her son her blue-eyed boy raped her daughter all she could say was im sorry but neither child understood why anything was wrong when becky explained they both left her so she was all alone

Alone.

Bereft.

Empty.

Even her fear abandoned her, leaving an empty shell, a husk, a harlot who bedded different causes, different philosophies, in the hope that they might fill the void within her but who had been cast aside now that the ideologies had finished with her.

She was nothing. Insignificant. Nothing she had done

had ever made any difference. All the good – the charity events, the anti-war rallies. All the bad – shoplifting as a kid; sending the police an anonymous tip falsely accusing her college boyfriend of selling drugs after he inadvertently made an anti-Semitic joke while stoned. None of it mattered.

She was all alone, lost even to herself.

Flotsam, jetsam. Spiritual debris. Her entire existence completely immaterial; hopes, fantasies, ambitions – all of them ghosts that never were. She was beneath note, beneath –

Stop.

Maybe she *was* worthless, her fears and dreams amounting to nothing more than meaningless hubris. But they had brought her here. She had defied Devereux, she had wept for the dancers, she had sacrificed herself. And all these actions had stemmed from a desire to protect the little girl, Lucy. It didn't matter if Becky didn't exist, she would not allow an innocent to suffer. All the different hopes and neuroses led back to that core truth, the essence around which her self was based.

The winds tore at her, stronger than ever, trying to break her. She faced them, proud, defiant. Reducing her to nothing had only served to reveal her inner core. She wrapped her personality around that core, reassembling her psyche piece by piece until she was whole once more.

The winds hurled her from the Abyss. She hit the ground, bounced, rolled to a stop inside a darkened cave. Her entire body ached; one big mass of lacerations and contusions. She lay there, groaning, not wanting to move for at least a couple of millennia.

A shadow fell across her and she squinted up at a tall figure who stood at the mouth of the cave. "Well, that was bracing."

Devereux.

He smoothed down a lock of golden hair that had fallen out of place during their ordeal. Otherwise he appeared completely unaffected, as radiantly flawless as before.

"I'm afraid you rather took the brunt of our little jaunt through the Abyss. Of course that was my plan all along. Just be grateful that I arranged for Choronzon, the master of that disagreeable little realm, to be occupied elsewhere otherwise things would have been become really unpleasant."

"Where's Rebecca?"

"When a person enters the Abyss his or her Holy Guardian Angel cannot travel with them. The Angel is stripped away, leaving the person to face the Qliphoth and their master Choronzon alone. But I felt that rather a foolish thing to do so I devised an alternative approach. By clinging to you and Rebecca as we entered the Abyss I was able to trick the Qliphoth into thinking that you and I were a single entity and so they were content to strip away just the one Holy Guardian Angel, leaving mine intact."

Becky rubbed her aching temple. She couldn't focus, she felt as though she had too many thoughts in her head. She wished Rebecca were here to help her make sense of all this. "You killed her."

"Actually, she's perfectly fine. Although Holy Guardian Angels can't traverse the Abyss they are reunited with their hosts on this side. She'll be along to join you at any moment. Which means I'm in rather a hurry to reach Kether. My plan will run a lot smoother if I don't have to contend with her interference."

He offered Becky his hand. "Shall we?"

She remained crouched in the cave's shadows. Perhaps if she could delay him long enough Rebecca would arrive to save her. "Why are you doing this?"

"To attain enlightenment. To draw back the veil that shrouds reality. To raise humanity out of the darkness and into the light."

Becky stared at him. "You're doing this for humanity?"

"Of course. Once I'm enlightened I shall share my knowledge with the world and usher humanity into a new aeon of peace and prosperity. Every man and woman will be free to unleash their desires and fulfil their potential." He smiled at her, his perfect teeth gleaming. "I bet you thought I was evil."

If it wasn't for the pain wracking Becky's body, all but paralysing her, she would have gouged his eyes out, leaving gaping sockets weeping blood. Instead she swallowed her rage. "These … desires. Are they going to be the kind of thing you're doing to me right now on earth?"

"I do apologise for that, but it's essential for the ritual. All for the greater good of course. And I do appreciate your sacrifice – 'It is a far, far better fuck than I have ever fucked before …'"

Again Becky fought back the desire to gouge out his eyes. The bastard actually thought he was being charming. "So you're only raping me to help humanity. You're not enjoying it at all?"

"I didn't say that. You're a very attractive woman. Besides, once the new aeon dawns outdated morality will be abandoned. Conventional thinking is a cage; people keep doing the same things, thinking the same ideas, simply because they are afraid. They are cowering in Plato's Cave, clutching at the shadows; I aim to show them the world outside. To free their bodies and their souls."

Becky frowned. Thoughts swirled in her head, refusing to come into clear focus. Part of her agreed with what Devereux was saying, but he was twisting the concept, perverting it. "So if this new unfettered morality allows people to rape they're going to need victims. Doesn't that invalidate your entire argument about bringing freedom?"

"There are always people willing to become victims. Given the right incentive." Devereux smiled at her. "You should know."

"If you're forcing them into the choice then it's not much of a choice is it?"

Devereux extended his hand. "If we are to continue this discussion we should do so while heading towards Kether." Sparks of flame danced around his eyes. "I really must insist."

Reluctantly Becky took his hand and allowed him to pull her to her feet.

"I would allow you to rest a little while longer, but as I said I want to get underway before your Holy Guardian Angel – "

Devereux broke off to stare at Becky.

She didn't understand what had so stunned him until she looked down to where he held her hand. Becky's skin was wrinkled and dotted with liver spots, her fingers stiff with arthritis. As she stood in daylight for the first time since crossing the Abyss her hair caught in a breeze and blew across her face. Black curls had turned grey. Breasts and belly sagged. Touching her withered hands to her face she felt jowls and a web of scars.

She and Rebecca had become one.

Her muddled thoughts began to clear slightly, new insights and knowledge gaining clarity as they slotted in alongside the old ones. It felt a little like when she learned to read and write; a whole new range of possibilities opened up to her. Or when, as a child, she had begun to grasp the difference between traditional and secular Judaism; her perspective of the entire world changed, gaining extra layers and nuances.

"Ah." Devereux smoothed his hair, regaining his composure. "Welcome back, my dear. This illustrates rather nicely a point I was about to make about subjugation leading to liberation. You would never have achieved this level of mastery if I had not ... motivated you."

"Climbing the Tree of Life made me stronger. You raping me just made me hate you."

A tiny flicker of hurt registered behind Devereux's arrogance. Becky pressed home her attack. "You might think it was some great act of liberating magic but you're just a pathetic misogynistic piece of shit."

Devereux flushed deeply, his crimson brow drawing into a scowl.

Grabbing her wrist Devereux flew up into the sky, dragging Becky along with him. She clung to him in terror. Whatever magical powers she might now possess they had not yet manifested and her returning future memories suggested that even if her powers were fully functioning the ability to fly was not among them.

As they rocketed into the black sky she stared down at a city of pyramids that stretched to each horizon. Outside each pyramid stood a cadaverous figure performing magic rituals. Becky sensed the silent chant emanating from the zombified figures, each claimed to be a different master of the mystic arts, but all of them looked exactly the same as they all performed exactly the same ritual: sawing a woman in half. They did not perform the trick in the traditional manner, cutting across the woman's body, instead they placed the saws' teeth in the slit of each woman's vagina and worked the blade back and forth, threatening to cleave the women lengthways. Wet mascara ran down heavily rouged cheeks as the women silently intoned "Oh baby, you're the best" – while all the time gazing downwards in an expression of infinite sorrow.

Becky followed their gaze and the ground turned transparent, revealing an image of Becky back on earth with Devereux rutting fiercely between her legs.

The golden haired Devereux who carried her through the air growled to his earthbound counterpart. "Slow down, you fool. I'm not there yet."

Invisible tendrils of regret and despair reached out to Becky. This was not how it was supposed to be. The women were supposed to have the power in this realm. But the men had taken it from some of them while others had given it up willingly, hoping for something better.

Becky wished she could do something to help the women. Although she had glimpses of insight into the world of magic she still did not fully comprehend how it worked. Perhaps she had not yet fully joined with Rebecca. Or perhaps there were limits to what a Holy Guardian Angel could do. It was possible that Rebecca's memories were not as useful as Becky hoped because Rebecca came from a different future to the one that would stem from current events. Or perhaps Rebecca wasn't really from the future at all; she was just a construct from Becky's imagination, the woman she wanted to be. And if that were true, what limitations did that place upon Rebecca? She obviously knew things that Becky didn't, but was she accessing buried memories or tapping into something else, something bigger?

Slowly the sky turned grey. Celestial spheres orbited above them. Orchids spread across the landscape. This plane had a different energy; here masculinity was in the ascendancy. But it was a broken masculinity; abusive boyfriends, absent fathers and chauvinistic bosses.

Becky felt a sense of panic build within her. An existential dread, a spiritual panic attack. A terrible emptiness ran through the whole of creation. Something was missing, something vitally important that she had always taken for granted but which now it was gone she realised she loved more than life itself.

Devereux felt it too. He looked round frantically, his smooth exterior cracking. "There's no God. There's supposed to be a God. Where's the fucking God?"

A temple appeared before them, standing proud in the middle of a vast wasteland. The temple's spires and brightly coloured stained glass windows were in sharp contrast to the sparse brown grass that resembled thinning hair; the river of bubbling testosterone; the scant trees made of twisted sinew, with shrivelled testicles dangling from their branches.

Devereux flew towards the temple, aiming for its huge oak doors. The doors remained shut. Devereux refused to change course. The doors filled Becky's vision, then the oak panels, then the grain of the wood. A split second before collision Becky thrust her hand forwards and a blast of dazzling energy blew the doors open.

Becky gasped. Her powers were real. She really had become her own Holy Guardian Angel. Now she just had to figure out what that meant.

She hadn't actually cast a spell; she still didn't know how. All she had done was throw her arms up to protect her face and wish the doors would open. Rebecca said that some of the magic Devereux used was based on things he had made up himself. Could Becky do that too? Was her imagination her greatest weapon?

Then she saw the interior of the temple and that took up all her attention.

The temple was huge, a gigantic monument to spirituality. Vast, ornate, magnificent.

And empty.

Becky and Devereux landed at its centre and stared about them. With the sound of scraping stone gargoyles and grotesques detached themselves from the walls, giggling as they tugged blocks free and slid them across the floor, reassembling them into a new wall. If they kept it up they would rebuild the entire temple a few feet from its original position. Judging by the scratches and grooves worn into the stone floor Becky guessed this wasn't the first time they had performed this task.

She bit her lip, her earlier panic turning to confusion. Whatever insights her bonding with Rebecca may have afforded her they did nothing to explain this place. She had hoped joining with her Holy Guardian Angel would answer all her questions, resolve all her doubts. Instead, greater knowledge led to greater mysteries. It was similar to how, as a child, she couldn't wait to grow up and become an adult so she could have all the answers and gain control of her life. Instead, despite her greater knowledge and experience she still found herself floundering in situations she didn't understand.

Beside her, Devereux looked equally bewildered; his brow knitted and his jaw twitched.

A shaft of light beamed through the stained glass window; the light split, cleaved by the prism of the glass, first into two beams and then into dozens, all of them different colours and intensities. The lights brushed Becky and her confusion deepened. Then she stared up at the light that shone in through the window. Pure, untainted: the one true light.

Devereux followed her gaze and his frown eased into a smile.

Becky felt a sense of confidence growing within her, a sense of rightness. She knew her path, knew her purpose in life. It felt so good, she had to shout it to the entire universe. Her entire being encapsulated within a single word. She shouted it aloud and it sounded beautiful.

At the same moment Devereux shouted too, his cry blending with Becky's so she could not make out what either of them had actually said. Yet somehow she knew that Devereux had uttered the exact same word as she, even as she knew that his understanding of its meaning was entirely different to hers.

She and Devereux floated upward, toward the light. No longer powered by Devereux's powers, just drifting gently. They glided through the window and into the light.

It was dazzling. Luminescent. A white brilliance that touched the soul. Becky wept tears of joy. They came not just from her eyes but from every pore in her body; ecstatic tears of the soul that joined with the white light.

Tears leaked from Devereux too. They spiralled around Becky's, tried to merge with them, but they were like water and oil.

Slowly, the white brilliance divided. A creature appeared, covered in scales, with two heads and huge bat-like wings. Leering, the creature pointed to Becky.

As Becky stared Devereux grabbed her, forcing himself inside her. She tried to push him away but she was helpless, his youthful body easily overpowered her frail, elderly frame. All she could do was stare in horror at his eyes as an image formed there, some kind of sigil; it forced her vision downwards, her gaze sliding down Devereux's body as if drawn by a great weight to his throat then to his throbbing genitals.

Then she saw her own eyes, throat and genitals. She blinked, her vision segmenting, two sets of images overlapping each other as she saw Devereux's view of events as well as her own. Then her vision multiplied again, she saw not only two views of the rape occurring in the spiritual realm but also the one occurring back on earth.

And it wasn't just the vision that she shared. She could feel the venom building in Devereux's scorpion-penis, but from this perspective it didn't feel like venom, it was unadulterated pleasure, pure animal passion, a radiant gift from the gods themselves. She experienced everything that Devereux felt.

Even better, he experienced everything that *she* felt.

The pain, the fear, the humiliation. All of it etched upon her face (or his face; they had swapped places after all). Tears and snot ran together; he was terrified, he didn't understand what was happening. (She didn't understand either, but she didn't care.) He begged for mercy; pathetic whimpers that choked off as they became actual words. (It sounded so wonderful, the sweetest of music.) He turned his face away, eyes tightly shut, trying to blot out what was happening, knowing that it wouldn't work, he would remember every detail forever. (Briefly, she wondered if she should stop, but tossed the thought aside. She couldn't stop now even if she wanted to. She was unsure of the source of this violent rage, whether it was Devereux's perversion or her own sense of vengeance or some strange combination of the two; whatever it was it had a hold of her now and she thrilled to its embrace, thrusting her hips harder and harder, building to climax, all the time screaming "This is what it feels like! This is what it feels like!")

And then she came.

The venom gushed from her, spurting in a joyous spray, filling a part of Devereux which he had never expected to possess. Devereux's eyes widened in shocked agony. His hands clawed at her feebly, pitifully. His hold around the scorpion loosened; not because the scorpion had turned flaccid but because its venom was eating through flesh, hollowing out his body. The pelvis melted away and Becky's hips bumped against the floor, then the ribcage dissolved and she slumped forward onto the mass of empty skin. Eyes leaked from sockets in a gooey mess, the skull dwindled to nothing. Finally, skin and hair dissolved.

Nothing remained. Not even a stain upon the floor.

Her physical embrace with Devereux at an end Becky jerked away from his spiritual embrace.

The mad rage subsided and she stared about her in horror.

She had no body to return to. She was trapped here

forever.

*

Sajid backed away from the monster. Slow. Cautious.

The monster changed shape, its body spinning and churning like Sajid's guts after a dodgy curry. Air crackled with jabs of forked lightning. Demon reeked of raw sewage drenched in cologne; a vicious one-two to the nostrils. It spoke again, a voice filled with insanity and psychosis and all other kinds of mad shit. Talking in at least six different languages at once, overlapping, muddling, confusing, arguing with each other – a demented free-for-all at the United Nations.

One voice cut through: "Who dares summon Choronzon?"

Dry mouth, dry tongue and heart stuck in his throat. Answer anyway, get this fucking freak off his back. "Not me, man. I ain't got nothin' to do with it. These other fuckers, they're the ones what called you."

An eye snaked out on the end of a stalk, twitching, getting an ID on Alex and Millicent. "They are no longer living. Neither is the one whose body I possess."

Eyeball shot a look at Sajid, turned into a mirror, throwing his frightened reflection back at him. "But you are still breathing. And you are part of this ritual."

"Nah, man. I don't know these people. I got nothin' to do with their sick shit."

"Really?" Reflection in the mirror came to life; Sajid being gang-raped by Ravi and his pals.

Sajid puked; scotch and mineral water splattered the floor.

"You were meant to be the vessel. You are mine by

rights."

"No! I-I – "

On the stage Devereux finally got his rocks off, body spasming, lips moaning. Becky's body melted, dissolving into a pool of liquefied bone and skin before vanishing altogether.

Sajid's gut had already puked itself empty; it tried puking again anyway.

Couldn't take much more of this.

His body ached, left arm hung limper than his dick. Moving his arm hurt – muscles fucked up? Nerve damage? His torn up arse screamed every time he moved. Standing hurt, walking hurt. Fucks knows if he'd ever be able to take a shit without his sphincter collapsing. This Choronzon fucker got any closer and he'd find out.

Islam said every person has an angel looking out for them. Also said they had a devil looking to screw things up. Fighting a turf war over a person's soul, their destiny. No prizes for guessing who was top dog today.

Choronzon's eye/mirror retracted back into its body, lost in the swirl of impossible anatomy. A rotting liver swung out on a set of strings, twitching and jerking like a puppet. Mouth opened in the liver: blackened teeth and diseased gums. A wave of toxic level halitosis burned Sajid's eyes. Blood seeped from around the decaying teeth.

"You belong to me. Your soul is my plaything."

Sajid trembled.

"You cannot deny this. You are bound by the rules of magick and the universe."

Teeth twitched in the liver's gums. No, not teeth: maggots. Hatching into flies, coloured wings blurred in motion; vibrating jewels. Legs trapped in the sticky mess of bleeding gums, permission for takeoff denied. Helpless, buzzing in rage and frustration.

"You are mine."

The buzzing grew louder.

"I will torment you beyond the limits of sanity. And then beyond the limits of insanity."

Louder.

"Your agony will outlive eternity."

The buzzing eclipsed everything, filling the entire world.

"But there is another way."

Silence. The flies stood still, the buzzing gone.

"I will relinquish my claim to you on one condition."

Sajid stared at Choronzon. Hope flared within him. He would do anything the bastard wanted. Eat his own shit, slice his ears off, superglue his dick shut. *Anything*.

The liver's lips curled into a smile.

"Give me the little girl."

*

Despair enveloped Becky, smothering her. She had no way home, no physical form to which she could return. Not even a corpse that she might somehow find the spell to reanimate – being a zombie wouldn't be so bad so long as she could find a way to stop her body rotting or seizing up with rigor mortis. But there was nothing. Not even a single atom.

And yet she felt grateful for the despair. It helped distract her from the revulsion she felt for herself.

Devereux deserved what she had done to him. The pain, the degradation – she was just repaying him the hurt he had heaped upon her. It was a simple matter of justice.

Except she had enjoyed it.

Not just the physical sensation – although that had been wonderful in itself, so different to her usual female orgasm, in some ways smaller, less encompassing, yet with a special intensity all its own – but the sense of power and dominance and rage. It was a sliver of Devereux's demented mind stuck inside her psyche, shifting, worming its way to the very core of her being. That horrific sense of jubilation had all come from him.

But what if it hadn't?

Beside her Devereux curled up into a ball, weeping. The tears didn't attempt to absorb into the white brilliance, they remained on his cheeks, as though his sorrow was too vital a part of him to be removed, too great to be assimilated into cosmic unity.

Becky scowled. She refused to feel sorry for him. He had brought this upon himself.

Above her the two-headed creature split into two separate entities. The first a giant figure with the head of a bull but a human body, stripped to the waist and besmeared with blood, clutching a little boy in one hand and a little girl in the other as flames raged about it. Beside it stood a huge red dragon, or perhaps a serpent, with seven heads and ten horns and a crown upon each head. As more and more of the dragon's coils writhed into view its tail tore stars from the sky and hurled them to the earth.

Then a third figure could be seen; a woman clad in a purple and scarlet robe that barely covered her nakedness. She rode upon one of the dragon's heads; brandishing a gold cup, brimming with obscene and filthy things – all the hate and horror in the world.

The monstrous creatures leaned forward in gleeful

anticipation, like ancient Romans at the Coliseum. To them emotional distress was a blood sport.

The despair within Becky refused to subside. Somehow she had to extinguish it, along with the rage and hatred that still smouldered inside her heart ready to flare into a conflagration as soon as she lowered her guard.

Devereux continued weeping. His whole body shook, pain emanating from him in waves, his hurt a tangible presence. Stains on his robe showed that he had soiled himself.

Slowly, Becky reached out and placed her hand gently upon his shoulder.

Above her the dragon and the god with the head of a bull stared down at her in consternation, then they swirled and blended together, fading into nothingness. For a moment the woman remained, her face twisted in agony, then the pain passed and a maternal smile crossed her features and her dress became the sun, the moon lay at her feet and a crown of twelve stars rested upon her head before she too faded back into the light.

Becky thought she caught one last glimpse of the crown, or perhaps a lotus blossom with more petals than she could count – no, a smiling face. Calm, compassionate; so vast that it encompassed the whole of creation. And then there was nothing but the white brilliance.

A moment of pure bliss.

Transcendent ecstasy.

Then:

Fluctuations in the light. Images and sensations bubbled up.

Visions of Cable Street. Jews and gentiles lining the streets to battle Oswald Mosley's Blackshirts. A 1930s police doctor riding along on her bicycle to her patients, a black medicine bag swinging from the handlebars. An 18th century rabbi standing outside the Great Synagogue of London as a nearby fire drew close; the rabbi wrote four Hebrew letters upon the pillars of the synagogue's doors then turned to face the flames; they came no closer.

Becky smiled. She realised now the word that she had spoken in the temple.

Love.

Love between husband and wife, parent and child, brother and sister, neighbour and neighbour, between every living being. It was the only thing that mattered.

Devereux saw it too, she could tell. His weeping stopped as he gazed at the images before him, his mouth gaping in slack-jawed wonderment. Slowly, a gleam came into his eyes. The images began to change.

The Jewish protestors hurling bricks, overturning a bus, fighting with the police – giving and receiving vicious beatings while Mosley and his Blackshirts took a detour to avoid the battle. A woman's butchered body lying upon a mortuary slab inside a church. The doctor from before, now without her bicycle, being buried by a collapsing building during the Blitz as bombers roared overhead. More bodies in the mortuary; a family of three – husband, wife and baby son – all of them with their heads smashed in by a hammer. Mini-skirted prostitutes tottering on high heels. Gangs selling drugs.

Devereux's view of love was based upon fear and pain. Doing whatever it took to get people to bow down to him in worship. In his perverted view love only ran one way: to him. If he didn't receive it he would lash out in pain and anger, forcing everyone to love him.

The images changed again, still centring on Cable Street but at the same time reaching out further, extending their influence. A Jewish gangster with a mole on his left cheek, bragging about how he battled Mosley's Blackshirts, but not everyone believed him. The doctor crawling from beneath the rubble, bandaging her broken ankle, then spending the rest of the night caring for the other casualties. A crowd baying for blood as a man's corpse was buried at a crossroads with a stake through his heart. An elderly Swedish man in powdered wig talking to the rabbi who saved the synagogue, discussing the differences and similarities between physical and spiritual love. The doctor, now an army officer treating patients in Calcutta; still, the name by which history would remember her was The Angel of Cable Street.

Becky felt a jumble of emotions as she viewed the images; joy one moment, revulsion the next. Beside her Devereux frothed at the mouth as his body rocked with convulsions.

Becky began to experience tremors running through her own body. Thoughts and feelings ran wild, intellect and passion threatening to throttle each other. She couldn't centre herself. Couldn't tell right from wrong.

Looking up Becky saw something shimmering through the brilliance that surrounded her; a negative light that shone both bright and dark. It formed a veil, no, *three* veils, more – except there weren't any at all, a multitude of nothingnesses: 0, 00, 000 …

Nothing
Nothing becomes
Nothing is
She sensed intelligence beyond the veils, concepts

and philosophies that completely eclipsed anything she had previously experienced, a whole new way of thinking, of *existing*. Good and evil no longer existed, such trivial concerns were beneath consideration, in their place was a totally alien ethical framework, at once both more edifying and more terrifying. It was too much to take in – synapses strained, neurones buckled – she had to look away to save her sanity.

Reeling, she gazed back down at the images before her. They no longer felt so bewildering. In fact, compared with the mysteries beyond the veils it now all looked ridiculously simple.

She saw glistening strands of energy connecting people and events, felt the tension as history and destiny and free will all fought against each other in a sea of contradictions. This was the true essence of existence. Not love. Not hate. *Life*.

She had understood this concept intellectually, had even experienced it firsthand, but now she truly *felt* it, the way that one event affected another, they all flowed together in one seamless whole; physical, mental and spiritual all forming the same entity, the same organism – the macrocosm tracing the microcosm, replicating it on a grander scale, the microcosm tracing the macrocosm, creating a more intimate portrait – masculine and feminine came together, uniting: here the woman was not a whore but a consort, the man not a demon but a god; now she knew how to explain it to everyone, she could reassure them that although humanity would always have its demons they could be tamed, domesticated, balanced out alongside joy and contentment to make life more bearable; she just had to tell people how; find a form in which she could manifest herself and distribute her findings to everyone, even Devereux – vile, disgusting Devereux; if he could just let go of his hatred perhaps he could help; he knew far more about the technical aspects of the Tree of Life than she, perhaps she could find a way for him to help spread her epiphany, except he was shouting now, his eyes wide, the irises glistening with insane glee as he screamed at the veils "I understand! I understand it all!" but how could he understand what lay beyond when he didn't even grasp what lay in the here, the now, his rage and hatred projecting a shield around him that prevented him from connecting with anyone or anything else, even the host of angels that appeared circling above him in baroque spirals; male and female, beautiful in their nakedness – an angel swept down towards him, light radiating from her wings, singing a symphony of the sublime, her naked breasts flattening against his chest as she embraced him; and then a new revelation blossomed within the one Becky was already experiencing: Devereux wanted to be absorbed into the white brilliance, to find the love he sought in a glorious annihilation of the self, his whole body relaxed as he awaited his reward for his mystical travails; the angel's embrace turned intangible as a ghost, as insubstantial as a sigh, arms slipping inside him, wrapping about his soul; light from the angel spread across him, not the white brilliance, not the strange negative light of the veils, a lilac glow, fragmented, broken: the light from the Abyss; the angel's feathers transformed to scales, fingers became claws, her singing became a terrible wailing; Devereux was sucked into the Tree of Death – Becky tried to grab him, anchor him in the brilliance with her but it was too late, he disappeared into the Abyss, swallowed up by the Qliphoth, his anguished scream echoing across the void;

Becky stared at the spot where he had been, unsure even in her transcendence whether she felt upset or glad and then she was falling, *falling*, drifting down towards earth, a leaf fluttering down from the Tree; a sudden fear gripped her, she had no body to which to return, surely without a corporeal form her spirit would evaporate, dissipating into the aether – before the fear could fully take hold she found herself drifting towards a body vacant of mind and soul, moreover, she knew to whom the body belonged: Devereux.

*

Sajid could walk out of there. Alive. Whole.

Just go. Don't look back. Don't stop for nothing.

It was the only thing to do. Anything else was crazy, full on mental, 100% certifiable.

Choronzon spun and swirled; limbs spiralling around, changing angles as they gained extra joints: a demonic break dancer. Body grew, extra mouths popped out all over, eyeballs sprouted clawed fingers.

No way Sajid could fight this freak.

Wouldn't mind so much if it was Iblis; least then he knew where he stood. He'd been an evil cunt and Iblis was making sure he paid for it. Be okay with that, at least he would be punished by the Islamic devil, in some way would still be connected to his religion, even in torment. But this *thing* – Allah had nothing to do with this. If this took him Allah had abandoned him, thrown him out, changed the locks, got a restraining order.

Fangs, tentacles, spiked tails, armour-plated legs: all writhed madly, spinning around and around. Looked like someone emptied a zoo into a washing machine.

Crazy to try and stop it. Suicide.

Sajid edged towards the door.

"You give the girl to me?"

He stopped. Giving up the girl meant giving up everything he had gained since prison. Self-respect. Redemption. Salvation.

Sweat all over him. Dripping off his lumpy nose and his beard, sliding down his back, slithering into his ruined arse. Each drop tickling him with its chills.

Cold as ice. Cold as his heart.

He nodded.

Laughter crackled round the strip club. Cruel. Gloating. Demented.

"Bring her to me."

Sajid hesitated. A scam: he brought the girl over and Choronzon wasted both of them.

He shook his head.

"Bring me the girl."

Another shake.

"Do not toy with me, little man. You have summoned up something you cannot put down."

Sajid stayed put.

"Bring her!"

Wrathful.

Commanding.

Desperate.

Something else was going on here, something important. Eyes narrowed, scanning Choronzon, the girl, the dancers, the triangle painted on the floor ...

Choronzon was inside the triangle. Swirly little bastard hadn't stepped outside it since showing up. Waved its arms about, but never actually touched anything. It couldn't. Fucker was all front.

Big gamble. If Sajid was wrong about this then everything went to hell. Literally.

Deep breath. Make peace with Allah.

"Get her yourself."

Choronzon was still. No wriggling, no writhing, no squirming around like an epileptic jellyfish. Perfect stillness.

"What?"

Even frozen like that still couldn't see what the bastard looked like. Its body swallowed Sajid's gaze, sucked it into some other dimension full of blackness and invisibility.

Don't matter. Give the fucker the drug dealer stare. The 'You're on my turf so don't be disrespecting me or I'll cut your fucking balls off' stare.

"I said get her yourself, innit?"

Choronzon started thrashing around again, swelling up to super-sized proportions. "I command you!"

"Go fuck yourself." Hard to tell with the way Choronzon's body parts spun about but it might already be doing that.

"You're stuck in that triangle, innit? You're trapped. Can't even touch nothin'. So don't be givin' me no orders."

Choronzon didn't answer.

Sajid turned; limped towards the door. Too fucked up to do anything else. He'd done his part. Let Five O or the paramedics sort this out. Let Choronzon throw a tantrum; he couldn't hurt anyone.

"There are other torments beyond the physical."

Sajid looked back; saw a stalk snaking over to the little girl, a mirror on the end. Horrible images flickered across the mirror's surface. "Insanity is just as cruel as flayed skin or a severed tongue."

The little girl turned; faced the mirror. Slowly; sleepwalking, or in a trance or something.

Ten metres away. Too far for Sajid to help her even if he wanted. Couldn't hobble over in time – Choronzon would just fry his brain before going on to the girl anyway.

Girl's eyes grew wide, drinking in madness. Choronzon cackled, triumphant.

Howled in pain as a tray smacked into the stalk, knocking the mirror aside.

Sajid snatched up another disc-shaped tray off a table, flung it like a Frisbee. Bounced off one of Choronzon's heads. Demon screamed. Lunged at Sajid, whipping the mirror of madness at his face. Pulled up short when Sajid grabbed another tray to use as a shield. Mirror swayed back and forth, trying to get past the tray. Sajid shifted, tracking it with his peripheral vision, not dumb enough to look straight on.

Couldn't figure out why the trays hurt Choronzon. Solid matter hurt a demon whose summoning ritual hadn't been completed? Symbols on the trays repelled it? Didn't matter. Too tired to keep dodging it. Going to catch a glimpse of the mirror, go insane.

Already insane. Fighting a demon with a fucking serving tray. Acting like a hero. Playing at religious convert. Just a street thug, looking to protect his turf, kill anyone who messed with him, unless they killed him first.

Giggled. Chuckled. Totally cracked up.

Choronzon flinched. Sajid laughed harder. Choronzon flinched again; screaming. The laughter hurt it more than the trays.

Hysterics now. Ready to piss himself. Poor little demon didn't like being laughed at. Must have been bullied at school.

Choronzon, shrank, dwindling down to nothing.

Empty triangle. Just a few wafts of smoke.

Girl stared at the wall, sane but still doped up to the eyeballs.

Sajid looked at her, the dancers, the dead bodies.

He stopped laughing.

Picked up the candlestick, red and sticky with Ravi's blood. He was no hero, he just wanted someone to kill.

Up on the stage Devereux stirred.

Sajid marched forward, hefting the candlestick.

*

Becky settled into Devereux's body and opened her eyes, taking in the club; as she had descended back to earth she sensed that the situation had changed here, even if it hadn't her new powers would help even the odds, so she wasn't too concerned until she saw Sajid about to cave her skull in with a candlestick, then she moved faster than she had ever moved in her life, rolling to one side and then springing to her feet, backing away quickly, ignoring the pain in Devereux's old knees and shouting "Sajid, it's me! It's Becky!" before realising that given the savage expression on his face and the blood dripping from his backside he probably wasn't in the best frame of mind to accept such a revelation, and even though she could freeze him in time or restrain him within a bubble of magical energy she thought it prudent not to test her powers on someone driven to murderous fury, it would only prompt yet more rage, so instead she altered the molecular structure of Devereux's body, shifting an X chromosome here and a Y chromosome there until she reverted to her own gender, her own body in fact, even if the raw materials were not quite the genuine article; the resulting metamorphosis had the result she had hoped for: Sajid lowered the candlestick and stared in open-mouthed wonderment; to ease his bewilderment she beamed her most beguiling smile – "It really is me" – which at first she thought had the desired effect but then Sajid's gaze turned from her to the bloodstained candlestick in his hand and he started to tremble, he dropped the candlestick in revulsion and stared at the dead bodies of Alex and Millicent; tears moistened his cheeks "By Allah, what did I *do?*"

Becky reached out a hand to comfort him and to explain the vision of interconnectedness she had witnessed and which she wished to share with humanity. But although the concepts remained in her head, forming a complete and beautiful picture, there were now seams joining the concepts together, turning the picture into a jigsaw.

She tried to smooth out the picture, to recreate its wholeness by analysing its structure, but that just divided it into thoughts.

She tried to explain it to Sajid, hoping that describing the picture aloud would anchor it in her mind, but that just divided it into words.

Desperate, she tried to cling to the picture. Reproduce it. Trace it.

The picture drifted further away. Details blurred, disappeared. She had to fill in the gaps, restore the wholeness. She could do it; it was possible. If she could just imagine it.

Sajid stared at her. "What are we even doing here?"

She knew that. She had an answer. Somewhere in her head she had an answer.

Please let her have an answer.

Sajid wept. "Do you understand any of this?"

It was fading.

Hold on to it.

Hold on.

"I-I think so."

"Explain it to me, yeah?" He grabbed her wrists, begging. "Enlighten me."

Hersham Horror Books

Biographies & Story Notes

Peter Mark May was born in Walton on Thames Surrey England way back in 1968 and still lives nearby in a place you've may now of heard of called Hersham. He is the author of *Demon, Kumiho, Inheritance* [P. M. May], *Dark Waters* (novella), *Hedge End* and *AZ: Anno Zombie*.

He's had short stories published in genre Canadian & US magazines and the UK & US anthologies of horror such as *Creature Feature, Watch*, the *British Fantasy Society's 40th Anniversary anthology Full Fathom Forty, Alt-Zombie, Fogbound From 5* and *Nightfalls*. His next short story will appear in Western Legends *The Bestiarum Vocabulum*.

Website: http://petermarkmay.weebly.com/

Story Notes:

Travel really does broaden the mind. While on holiday in Tunisia a few years ago I bought one of those little guide books about the country, which gave a brief overview of the country. The ancient world always intrigues me, and it told of the destruction of Carthage the mighty city of Hannibal during the Punic Wars. So I read a book called *The Fall of Carthage* by Adrian Goldsworthy to add to my knowledge.

I found it interesting that once the city had been captured by the Romans, it was sacked, its women and children sold into slavery and the buildings razed to the ground. The earth had then been ploughed and salted to prevent crops growing there again.

My mind though, deemed it was salted for a very different reason....

Thana Niveau is a Halloween bride who lives in a crumbling gothic tower in the heart of Wicker Man country. (Otherwise known as the Victorian seaside town of Clevedon.) She shares her life with husband and fellow horror scribe John Llewellyn Probert, in a gothic library filled with arcane books and curiosities.

She can trace her love of gothic horror to her ninth birthday, when her mother gave her a book of stories by Edgar Allan Poe. "The Tell-Tale Heart" became her favourite bedtime story, one she demanded to hear again and again. More than any other single thing, the beating of that "hideous heart" made her want to be a writer.

She is the author of the short story collection *From Hell to Eternity*, published by Gray Friar Press. Her stories have been reprinted in *The Mammoth Book of Best New Horror (volumes 22, 23 and 24.)* Other stories appear or are forthcoming in *Exotic Gothic 5; The Burning Circus; Sorcery and Sanctity: A Homage to Arthur Machen;*

Steampunk Cthulhu; Sword & Mythos; Bite-Sized Horror 2; The 13 Ghosts of Christmas; Magic: an Anthology of the Esoteric and Arcane; Terror Tales of the Cotswolds; The Black Book of Horror (volumes 7, 8, 9 and 10); Death Rattles and Delicate Toxins.

Her online lair is thananiveau.com and you can also stalk her on Facebook.

Story Notes:

The seed of *"Little Devils"* had been rattling around in my head for a while. I love horror with children as the central characters and I had this nebulous idea of a devil worship ritual involving kids who didn't really know what they were doing. So that's the idea I ran with when Stuart invited me to submit a story for his Dennis Wheatley tribute anthology.

I didn't want to do a pastiche, as that could so easily turn into parody. (And bless him, but dear old Dennis is easy to poke fun at!) Fortunately, Stuart said it didn't have to be in Wheatley's style; it just had to involve demons or devil worship. So I had a bunch of Wheatley-era posh kids stumble on an incomplete Satanic ritual and inadvertently summon something evil. I liked the idea that the summoned demon could decide whether the sacrifice made in its name was worthy or not. If not, it could choose another. And I tried to make the kids horrid enough that you wouldn't feel too sorry for them. It could easily be a 1970s public information film about the dangers of building sites. I'm sure Dennis would have approved.

John Llewellyn Probert is the author of the Amicus anthology tribute collections *The Faculty of Terror and The Catacombs of Fear* (both published by Gray Friar Press), as well as *Coffin Nails* (Ash-Tree Press) and his latest, *Wicked Delights* (Atomic Fez,) which received a starred review from Publishers' Weekly. Find out about them all at www.johnlprobert.com. He is the recipient of over twenty 'Honorable Mentions' from Ellen Datlow's *Year's Best Horror* series in all its forms, and he received the Dracula Society's Children of the Night award for *The Faculty of Terror*. His latest book is the crime novella *Bloody Angels* (Endeavour Press). Coming soon is a magic realism novella, *Differently There* (Gray Friar Press). *The Little Book of House of Mortal Cinema*, a volume of his film reviews, will be forthcoming from Pendragon Press in October. His next anthology appearances will be in *Psycho-Mania*! (Robinson), Exotic Gothic 5 (PS Publishing), World War 2 Cthulhu (Cubicle 7), and *The Tenth Black Book of Horror* (Mortbury Press). He is married to the horror writer Thana Niveau, and is currently at work on the sequel to his Spectral Press novella, *The Nine Deaths of Dr Valentine*, as well as a new novel and another short story collection. He rarely sleeps.

Story Notes:

Where do you begin if you're asked to do a devil worship story? For me, those two words conjure up a heady mix of Dennis Wheatley; Italian Exorcist rip-offs filled with nudity and ludicrous plots; and comic books from my youth, especially the UK Pocket Chiller Library series No.112 entitled '*Everlasting Night'*, which was about a pretty young thing who goes to work as the secretary for a Jason King-type author (judging by his hairstyle and clothes) in a remote country house. The scene where she discovers her predecessor lying next to an altar, her face torn off, one eyeball intact and a few wisps of hair still adherent to her scalp, is a piece of artwork that has haunted me from the age of eight. In fact it was that scene that inspired me to start writing Devil In The Details. It was intended to be a serious tale about a dead girl's vengeful spirit, with a ridiculous body count and no-one left alive at the end. However, it had been a long time since I had written a short story as fun as this one, and so I shouldn't really have been surprised when this wanted to be a lot lighter and humorous than I first anticipated. There aren't enough stories about what really goes on in Wales, anyway, so I hope this sheds some light on the matter.

David Williamson has been writing horror for several years. He was first published in *The 28th Pan Book of Horror* way back when, followed by three tales appearing in the *30th Pan,* one using the cunning pseudonym William Davidson.

He has also been in The *$5^{th}/6^{th}/7^{th}/8^{th}/9^{th}$* and soon to be published *10th Black Book of Horror*, Hersham Horror's *Alt-Zombie*, four different horror anthologies from Cruentus Libri Press and most recently, *Horrific History* from Hazardous Press. They will also shortly be publishing his first stand-alone collection, *Herbert Manning's Psychic Circus and Other Dark Tales.*

He is also due to appear in at least three other anthologies during 2013.

He lives on the South Coast of England, enjoys hiking across the Downs, real ale and playing his guitar…very, very badly.

Story Notes:

I have always loved Dennis Wheatley's writing, so when Peter Mark May told me he hoped to publish a Wheatley tribute anthology, I knew I had to try to be in it!

I had, at the time, been reading about Elizabeth I's England, and the real life characters of Doctor John Dee and his mysterious 'assistant' Edward 'Ned' Kelley cropped up several times along with their somewhat dubious practises. Dee was, amongst other things, the Queen's Astrologer but it was claimed that there was a much darker side to him and his interests.

I have no idea how other people write or come up with *their* tales, but I tend to absorb random bits of information that interest me and leave them to 'cook' (for want of a better word) in my head until the complete story is ready to be written. This process can take days or weeks…there seems to be no set pattern. More often than not, the story actually takes shape as I write it and once the bare bones are laid down, I go back over it several times to fine tune until I'm as satisfied as any author ever is with their work.

Stuart Young is a British Fantasy Award winning writer. His stories have appeared in magazines and anthologies such as *Catastrophia, Where the Heart Is, We Fade to Grey, Alt-Dead, Alt-Zombie* and *The Mammoth Book of Future Cops*. He has published three short story collections, with a fourth, *Reflections in the Mind's Eye*, forthcoming from Pendragon Press. He writes a column, *Sparking Neurones*, for the website *The Teeming Brain*. He keeps a blog at http://stuyoung.blogspot.co.uk/ *Demons and Devilry* is his first foray into editing. He's actually quite shy and nowhere near as demented as you might think from reading his fiction.

Story Notes::

FIVE FUN FACTS ABOUT GUARDIAN DEVIL*

*In this instance "fun" can also be interpreted as "dull," "tedious" and "downright infuriating."

1) I only edited the book because Peter Mark May was too lazy to do it. All I did was ask if I could submit to the anthology and the next thing I knew I'd been lumbered with organising the whole thing.

2) Although Dennis Wheatley is an influence on the story he's not the only one. William Hope Hodgson – a strong influence on Wheatley – was also rattling around inside my head. As were Mickey Spillane, James Ellroy, Joss Whedon, Grant Morrison, Alan Moore and a whole bunch of other authors. Unfortunately they all refused to do any of the actual writing. Bastards.

3) The story's setting came about from someone at my day job reminiscing about living near Cable Street. This piqued my interest and some quick research revealed that part of the East End to be the perfect setting for a story about the occult. Even better, several historical events tied to the area suggested themes for the story and saved me having to strain my brain coming up with ideas.

4) Guardian Devil was only supposed to be a short story. Unfortunately I got a bit carried away and it ended up being a novella. Where's a decent editor when you need one?

5) The story came about because I'd been reading about magic: the history, the concepts, the practitioners. So when I learned about the anthology it was the perfect opportunity to make use of my reading. Guardian Devil is mainly based around Qabalistic concepts and symbolism, some of which I've tried to recreate as accurately as I could from my research material, and others which I quite frankly made up in order to make the story flow more smoothly. I justify this cavalier attitude by citing the way many occult practitioners admire the manner in which Kenneth Grant never let such piffling details as facts get in the way of either his fiction or non-fiction writings on the occult. In doing so he produced work that many consider to have a more authentic occult feel to it than other writers who stuck more closely to the truth. (N.B. Pointing out that at least some of the symbolism in Guardian Devil is not of authentic occult origin relieves me of any responsibility if you should accidentally conjure up a demon while reading the story.)

Demons & Devilry

Fogbound From 5, Alt-Dead, Alt-Zombie. Siblings, Anatomy of Death, Demons & Devilry

all © Hersham Horror Books 2013

The Abhorrent Man © Peter mark May 2013

Little Devils © Thana Niveau 2013

The Devil in The Details © John Llewellyn Probert 2013

The Scryer© David Williamson 2013

Guardian Devil © Stuart Young 2013

Hersham Horror Books

Coming 2014 from

Hersham Horror Books

HORROR AMERICANA

JOE MCKINNEY'S
FAVOURITE HORROR STORIES OF THE 20TH CENTURY

http://silenthater.wix.com/hersham-horror-books#

Made in the USA
San Bernardino, CA
06 December 2013